RUTHLESS LIES

KINGS OF EDEN

BOOK THREE

MILA YOUNG

HARPER A. BROOKS

DEDICATION

For all our readers who love chaos before their happily ever afters....

Love you all
Mila and Harper

CONTENTS

KINGS OF EDEN SERIES

Kings of Eden

Stolen Paradise

Ruthless Lies

The dark secrets of my past might just be the end of us...

For a long time, I thought I knew who I was, but I've never been more wrong in my life. My father, the Horseman of War, found me. He's a ruthless, blood-thirsty tyrant, and as far as he's concerned, the two of us can't be alive at the same time. So, guess who he's coming for?

I'm running out of time.

My Kings will fight with teeth and claws to protect me, but what if it's not enough? What if the men who gave me their hearts will perish because of me?

I have no idea if any of us will survive...

This final fight will be our sought-after salvation, or a savage end to the love I've finally found.

CHAPTER ONE

EVE

"Knox!" Cassius barks beside me. His grip tightens on my shoulder. "Are you out of your fucking mind?" His body is vibrating so violently, the demon twisting his handsome features, he's not even trying to fight it anymore. "I don't want to kill you, but I will if I have to."

Dracon's gaze switches between the other two apocalypse horsemen. "We'll kill them all."

Brone's laughter rises, the horrible wheezing sound making goosebumps rise on my skin. "At least these mortals are good for a laugh," he says to Opia, but she doesn't look amused in the slightest.

Knox is still staring at me, his expression too hard to read. It's a mess of conflicting emotions.

Part of me is destroyed that he's so willing to just give me up to be slaughtered, especially after everything we've been through. But the other part is worried about the war that'll ensue between the Kings and the horsemen if they try. He can't really be okay with this.

He can't.

Brows pinching, he breathes, "Little dove..."

He says it as if it pains him, and I can see that pain shining in his hazel eyes.

"Knox, p—please..."

He doesn't say anything.

"Well?" Brone presses. "What are you waiting for? Dispatch this abomination's soul from her body, or I will. Let's be done with it."

Another second drags on, feeling like an eternity, and still Knox's eyes stay locked on me.

"Knox," Dracon growls. "Don't you fucking dare. Cassius—"

Cassius nods, agreeing with Dracon's silent command. "We'll take you out, man. We will. Don't make us do it."

The tension is thick between us, Knox, and the two other horsemen, but no one moves for a few more moments.

Then, Knox spins back around, wet hair whipping around his face, and steps between us and Opia's pointed blade. He raises his hands, and the shadows spread over the dock rise up like they had with Aris, and wrap their ghostly forms around Opia's arms. They tether her to the ground, making her sword unmovable.

Grunting, Opia struggles, her horse even trying to rear up and break their hold, but Knox's strange power is too strong.

"Knox!" Brone's raspy voice shouts in anger, but before he can retaliate, more shadows shoot up and bind his wrists too. He yanks and tugs at the binds, but to no avail. His voice booms against the night. "How *dare* you!"

"You are choosing to stand against us?" Opia says with raised brows.

"If you want Eve, you'll have to go through me," Knox growls, head tilting to the side like a serial killer regarding how to dice up his next victim. It's so disturbing, shivers shoot down my spine. "And every damned soul under my command."

Wait a fucking minute... Did he say, damned soul?

I study the strange dark things holding Famine and Pestilence, and as realization hits, so does the sickly feeling in my stomach.

Those aren't shadows Knox has been manipulating. They're souls. Spirits.

"We will kill Aris," he tells them in a firm voice. "Eve will take his place. Balance will then be restored."

Wait, what?

I almost fall over from his words. Or maybe it's from the blood loss and my adrenaline dipping—it's hard to tell. But Cassius's hand on me keeps me steady.

"Is there an echo in here? That's what I said," Cassius mumbles as he glances at Dracon. "Why does no one fucking listen to me in this group?"

Brone laughs even harder, the breathy bursts more like sharp gasps now. "You want to kill War?"

"I am Death, am I not?" Knox replies.

"Then where is your Mortem Scythe?" Opia's hard gaze drops to Knox's hip, looking for it.

The muscles in Knox's temples jump as he grinds his teeth. "That bastard tried to destroy it when he tried to kill me and threw me onto this plane. I was able to save a piece and fashion it into a blade."

"Then, where is it?" she demands with more power injected into her tone. "If you claim to want to kill Aris and replace him with this...this..."

"Abomination," Brone spits, revulsion curling his lip.

"*Eve*," I correct with venom, but Opia doesn't miss a beat.

"—then you will need the only weapon that can end one of our lives to do it," she finishes. "So then, where is it?"

A tense silence settles over the harbor. No one wants to reveal the truth. We're all still in shock from it ourselves.

Slowly, the shadowy tethers unwind from the two horsemen and sink back into the dark spots of the docks.

Now free, Brone rubs his wrists in annoyance. "Well?" The single word booms like a gunshot against the stillness.

"Aris took it," Knox replies finally. His fury is making the unruly shadows dance around him. "He has it."

Both Opia and Brone's eyes widened.

"War has the scythe?" she gasps, touching the sheathed sword at her hip.

Brone shakes his head. "No, no, no. This is not good..."

"You fucking think?" Cassius mutters what we're all thinking.

"With Death's scythe...he can't be stopped," Opia says. "Existence is doomed."

Cassius points to me. "Hey! She's Aris's daughter. And we're the most powerful creatures on earth, so if anyone can stop him, we can."

Yeah, right. Because we did such a fine job tonight?

Brone rolls his eyes. Or, I think that's what he did. It's hard to tell, with how foggy his irises are. "Your time on this plane has softened you, Knox. Has distorted your views."

Knox pauses, and although his chin rises, I see a flash of hurt in his eyes. I know he never wanted to be here on Earth—he was forced into it and into joining the Kings. He doesn't like interacting with humankind, so I'd be foolish to think anything else. No matter who my father is.

"I have learned a lot," he says instead. "I have done what I need to survive."

"Yeah," Cassius throws back at Opia and Brone. "It's not like you two came looking for him. We gave him a home. And plenty of bastards to kill. So maybe get off your high horses and think of a better way to help us then the whole lot of nothingness you've been spewing."

Brone's lip curls up in disgust. "We kill the girl, as suggested before. Restore the balance."

"Aris is going to come for you, whether Eve's dead or

not," Dracon says, stepping forward to regain control of the conversation again. "He has the Mortem Blade, and that means he can kill anyone."

I see where Dracon is going with this. "The guy's a psychopath. You don't think he's going to come after you two next?"

Opia glances at Brone. Worry wrinkles her beautiful features.

"Aris wants to rule over everything. He doesn't give a fuck about balance," Dracon goes on. "He needs to be stopped, and we can help."

"You know how dangerous he is with my blade, Opia," Knox says. "Even though she is half mortal, Eve is powerful. We can use her to help us defeat him and get my blade back. Restore the balance."

I don't know if I like being talked about like I'm a weapon. Or like I'm not standing right here, but I'm not an idiot. This is way beyond gangs and underground crime. These are powerful cosmic beings who've been alive for longer than I can wrap my head around. I'm more out of my element than ever here.

So are Dracon and Cassius, honestly, but they seem to have no problem challenging Pestilence and Famine to defend me.

"Very well," Opia says after a long pause, which wins her a baffled look from Brone. "It is certain Aris will come back for his spawn, whether to recruit her or destroy her himself."

"And we will be prepared and waiting," Dracon replies.

"You will all die. Aris is born in war and bloodshed." Brone throws another skeptical look toward his horsemen comrade. It's clear he's unsure what her motives in this are, and I'm not sure about them either.

"And I am the master of death," Knox says.

"Without your scythe, you are *weak*."

Knox's hazel eyes glow more yellowish-green in the dark as he narrows them.

Opia ignores the two and sets her attention on me, Dracon, and Cassius. "If you're willing to take the risk and face Aris here—on Earth—you should be able to defend yourself and your plane from that threat."

Dracon bows his head. "Thank you."

"We will use our resources to try and find him on our end. If Aris or his horse crosses over, they'll be greeted by us."

"And if we find Aris? Then what?" I ask, voice shaking just at the thought of facing that monster again.

"Take back the scythe and kill him before he kills you. It is the only thing that can stop him," she says.

"Easy." A devilish grin begins to spread Cassius's lips at the thought of our troubles finally ending with Aris dead. I don't blame him either—it is a tantalizing thought. But I may be the only one worried about the steps it'll take to get to that end goal.

And the amount of blood that'll most likely have to be spilled…

Me and Opia, that is, because her hard, concerned expression never wavers as the sky above us sparks with light and cracks open once again.

"Then you better do it, and do it fast, because with the Mortem Blade..." Opia tugs on her pale horse's reins and turns it in a circle, showing us her back as she readies to leave. Brone follows suit. "Aris won't stop until he kills us all."

CHAPTER TWO

EVE

"Eve, can we talk?" Knox asks, which is unlike him to actually ask. He's the kind of man to burst in and do as he wants. But after the confrontation with Aris, and the other horseman, we barely exchanged words on our way back to the Kings' Tower…where I reside and hid. For now…

I blink a few times, glancing over at Knox, who steps onto the balcony with me. Sunlight glints in his sorrowful eyes, the ache behind them changed from what I'd seen during our battle.

Something about him feels different—his expression, his deflated posture. It's like he's finally going to admit to doing the wrong thing, and now it's time for him to make up for it.

I grind my jaw, my gaze narrowing on his approach.

His mouth opens with his excuse…

"I'm not in the mood," I cut him off, then turn my back to him and sweep my gaze across the busy street below. At the cars in gridlock, the people rushing along the sidewalk, and the chaos of their simple lives. I forget what it's like to be just an ordinary person and I doubt I'll ever be that again after everything I've seen and experienced.

Knox remains near; I feel his stare on my back, and the hairs on my nape rise.

"You have every right to hate me," he begins.

I exhale loudly.

"You know what the saddest part is about betrayal? It's that it rarely comes from your enemy. Those closest to us always hurt us the most because they never realize what they have until it's too late." My voice quivers, and I hate that I can't still my emotions when anger ripples over me.

A sharp ache flares across my arm from where I was grazed by a rogue bullet, enough to draw blood and hurt like hell when I disinfected it. Now, each time it smarts, I'm reminded of how everything around me is crumbling.

Knox studies me, and my heart aches because I had started to fall for him, to tell myself that he actually cared. Turns out, I'm an idiot after all. And despite that, standing in front of him, it's impossible to ignore how my body hums in the company of this tall, dark, and dangerous as fuck horseman.

Wind blows past us, his black hair fluttering over his shoulder, his dark-rimmed eyes staring at me, irises so intense, I wonder if he's about to shed a tear. Instead, he rubs his fingers across the shadow of a beard along his strong jaw.

"I fucked up," he admits.

"You sure did. So, what do you want me to do? To accept your apology then all will be dandy? Well, I can't do that, so save your breath."

I move my attention back to the traffic below when Knox comes and stands by the railing, glancing at me.

Neither of us say a word, and the air thickens, but the longer we stay there, the harder it becomes to breathe as emotions choke me. The burning pain of him selling me out sits like a boulder on my chest.

"Just tell me one thing," I murmur.

"Anything." He gasps the word like it's a lifeline.

"Why'd you sell me out?" I turn to face him, wanting to see the answer on his face.

His head bows slightly, shadows gathering under his eyes. "I don't have a straightforward reason."

"Try," I grumble, my breaths speeding up, muscles tense.

"From the first time I saw you, I couldn't decide if I should kill you or fuck you. But it definitely swayed on the side of ending you."

"Oh, you're doing a great job so far of getting my sympathy." Of course, I knew what he'd told me because he'd tortured me down in his morgue room, but that was so long ago, I assumed we'd gotten over the whole butcher-me stage.

His jaw clenches as he swallows hard. "I started feeling

things for you that I tried to resist, but I was fucking lost to you, even if I refused to admit to myself. Then, when we faced the horseman, my mind wasn't screwed on right, the fire of battle raging in my veins, and I had a horrendous lapse of judgment. Fuck, but I hate myself for it. I can't even make a damn excuse for it because I had gone into autopilot where I only thought of myself, which was how I had survived when I worked closer with the horsemen. Emotions made you weak—Opia had always told me."

That has to be the longest I've ever heard Knox speak in one breath. The hurt in his eyes, the remorse behind his voice told me he's being sincere. And yet, it didn't tamp the flames of fury in my chest.

"I'm sorry, Eve. I'll do whatever it takes to show you how furious I am with myself, how I want nothing but to protect you. I'm fucking falling so fast for you that it scares me, but what terrifies me more is the idea of losing you."

"Well, there's nothing to worry about because we were never an item to begin with, so you'll get over it." The coldness of my response surprises me, considering I'm dying on the inside, my throat constricting as I draw back my emotions.

I push to get away from him, my eyes stinging with the promise of tears, but he grabs my wrist, pausing me. "Eve, don't leave. I can barely stand myself, and it's destroying me that I put you in danger. That I betrayed your trust."

Blinking back the tears, I twisted back around toward him where he's getting to his knees, and the hard shell I wrapped myself up in shows the first signs of cracking.

"For too long, I told myself I didn't need anyone. When I moved in with Dracon, I learned how to trust him, to know that he and Cassius weren't my enemy. But never in a million years would I have expected you to crawl under my skin and into my heart. So, what the hell would I do without your smiles, your smart-ass comments, your kisses. I won't be alright, and I'm drowning so fast, that I'm going to lose my fucking mind."

"What you did was a shitty thing, even for you." I pull my hand free from his grip.

He just stares at me with huge, startled eyes, showing me the real him for the first time—the vulnerable man who's always tried to be so strong that it backfires.

"Tell me what to do to make this better? I'll grovel for as long as you want me to. I'm sorry for trying to get you killed." His voice cracks. "And you were right. It wasn't until today that I realized that nothing else matters if you're not with me."

My knees wobble as his words flare over my mind. Knox doesn't do emotions and he's laying it on thick, but part of me can't help but think he isn't lying. I stare deeply into those beautiful hazel eyes, and I can't ignore the agony behind them.

"I don't mince my words, you know this. But I don't want you to doubt me when I'm pouring my heart out to you. When I have to show you how sorry I am, how I will make it up to you." He takes a small knife from his belt, which has me gasping and freaking out.

"W-What are you doing?"

"I'm going to show you that every time you doubt me, I'll bleed for you so you have no doubts." He pressed the sharp edge to the inside of his arm.

My heart slams into my ribcage and I lunge forward, my instinct taking over, grasping his hand with the knife. "Don't do that." Stunned, I don't release him, and he doesn't fight me either.

His eyes brighten, his mouth smiling weakly. "You still care for me, so there's hope."

"I just don't want you to do something stupid."

"Then give me time to make it right to you." His huge gaze pleads with me. "That's all I ask."

Shaking, I want this fixed and I hate confrontations, but seeing Knox keeps reminding me of his betrayal. Yet I also know that I don't want to lose him, which means we need a starting point for my heart to heal.

"I'm not ready to forgive you," I admit truthfully. "But I'll give you time to show me you're being truthful." My voice croaks and my cheeks are burning, hard to ignore the pain still cutting through me. Despite it all, I fight the urge to give in to him. I learned long ago that being the nice person gets you walked over, especially by those close to you. So, I'm happy for Knox to keep sweating and suffering a while longer.

He lifts his chin, staring up at me as he remains on his knees. "Thank you"

Without waiting a second longer, I tear out of

there, needing alone time to just process everything I've gone through. The close calls, betrayal, the uncertain future.

A shiver rips through me, and I hurry to my room, not seeing any of the other Kings along the way. Once I'm in my room, I press my back to the door and exhale loudly, letting out all the agony and fear and anger stored up within me.

Hiccuping my next breath, I wipe the tears that refuse to stay at bay. I'm a complete mess, and I don't know where to begin dealing with the danger we're all in. With the emotions tearing me on the inside, I'm unable to stop going over that Knox's initial instinct was to let me die.

And now he wants forgiveness, just like that?

What the fuck am I supposed to do with that?

DRACON

Moonlight pours into the room, the silvery hue glinting against everything it touches. I stir in bed, rolling over to the bedside table where the clock flashes three a.m.

Heart thundering, I flop onto my back, the still air doing nothing to cool me down. In truth, I hadn't switched on the air conditioner in my room, only had the window opened. My Apex beast inside me sometimes thrives on warmth, my dragon animal craving overwhelming heat.

Not that it's helped tonight. My past and present are colliding like an explosive bomb going off in my mind.

We should have finished off Aris, should have used the confrontation to end him, except I fucked up. Just as I'd done with Saxon...my best friend, my family... and got him killed because I couldn't get to him in time. I made the wrong decisions, which ultimately led to his death.

His blood is still on my hands, and the guilt strangles me.

I gasp for air and shove myself to my feet. I'm fucking burning up, and nothing's helping cool me down.

The thing is, I got my friend killed, and I almost got Eve and my men killed. And they don't say it, but they are thinking the same thing.

Moving to stand by the open window, I heave in lungful after lungful of air as I stare down into the night of the silent city. The occasional flutter of a breeze brushes over my naked body and does little to cool the inferno inside me.

"Saxon," I mumble under my breath. "If you were still with us, things would have been different." He'd always had his head screwed on right to see problems before they happened. We worked as a team, and nothing got past our defenses.

Now, I barely held onto control as my empire rattles around me, these fucking horseman threatening to tumble it over. They'll destroy it all if we don't destroy Aris first. And they'll take Eve with them.

I can barely breathe even as I stick my head outside. Sorrow and fury twist around me like barbed wire, tightening a bit more each day. Drowning, I push away from the window and head out of my room. My skin feels too tight, my head too foggy, and my broken heart too heavy.

With each step through the house, the images of Saxon lying in a puddle of blood suffocate me. If I hadn't pushed him on a job, a routine hit, he'd be alive now. But, like today, I'd been too fucking arrogant to see that we weren't untouchable, that death came for us all.

I shake my head, having told myself such thoughts will only screw me over, but tonight I'm floundering as the noose of what's coming for us lowers over our heads.

Suddenly, I'm standing in front of Eve's bedroom and pushing open her door. She could have died today…and it breaks every inch of my sanity to think of losing her.

Until she entered my life and her body invaded my thoughts—curvy and delicious—my world was a revolving door of misery and blood. I killed whoever got in my way, and only when I took a life did I feel a sliver of something in my black heart.

Fuck, now I spend endless nights inhaling her scent and picturing her naked and on my cock.

My steps are automatic as I enter her room, my gaze sweeping her bed. She has the blankets kicked off to the floor, and my beautiful girl lays on her back, completely naked, one knee bent, offering me the most beautiful view.

The faint moonlight drenching the room is all I need to easily make out the soft lips of her bare pussy, with just a sliver of her pink showing.

Heart in my mouth, my cock grows impossibly hard in moments, and my earlier worries are trumped by a rising tempo of arousal. Moving to stand at the end of her bed, I stare down at Eve's nakedness, my erection thick and upright like a pole.

My pulse is a roar in my ears and the heat of desire punches through me.

I want to deny the thoughts pouring over my mind of what I'd like to do to her.

I really should deny it.

But tonight I'm weak, and Eve is exactly what I need to soothe the anger and fury burning me from the inside out.

I kneel on the mattress and crawl between her legs, purposefully taking long movements in an attempt to awaken her. I'm on my stomach, my head deep between her thighs, face-to-face with her pussy. Inhaling deeply, her feminine, musky, sexy scent has my balls tightening.

I've fucked lots of women in my time, but none them had me as addicted as Eve. Her pussy might as well be a goddess, because I'm ready to worship her every day.

Glancing up, I see her breathing remains steady, her gorgeous breasts tempting me to reach over and tug on her nipples. Instead, I reach to her offering in front of me and pry open her lips, revealing her cute little clit and her hole that waits for me.

I lean in and run my tongue over her pussy, my eyes locked on my doll, wanting her awake so we can fuck. Shuddering at her honeyed taste, I close my mouth over her sweet cunt and devour her. Slurping and tugging on her lips, I can tell she's enjoying it as her hips are moving, her legs spreading for me.

Eve burns in my memory as the delicious warmth of her pussy embraces me.

Looking up at her body, her breathing increased, though she's still appears to be asleep. She's about to find out how real I can make her fantasy dreams. I bury my nose deep into her, taking her scent into me, and my beast growls in my chest.

A gasp rolls past her lips, and I plunge my tongue into her hole, pushing her legs wider. I want her to spread it for me and give me full access.

I push two fingers into her and her core clenches around them. She's drenched, so ready for me.

Lifting my gaze, I find her lazily opening her eyes and staring down at me.

"Hello, beautiful," I murmur, licking her slick from my lips. "How did you sleep?"

"I was having the most incredible dream of someone licking my pussy." Grinning, she pushes herself up onto her elbows, clearing her throat. "Are you having fun down there?"

"Would you like me to stop?" I pull back up and rest

on my heels, her attention dipping down to my now agonizingly hard cock.

"I'll be super pissed if you don't finish what you started."

A pulse jostles down to my dick where precum drips from the tip. Palming it, I tug on the flesh a few times. "Is this what you want?" I hiss.

Eve spreads her legs wider, rocking her hips higher, offering herself to me completely. "You're everything I want."

Inch by inch, I crawl over her, caging her with my body, my cock finding the hole that belongs to me in mere seconds. "You're so wet for me... Are you ready to suck down on my cock?"

She collapses onto her back, her breasts bouncing, her nipples hard. "You have no idea how much I need this release. Fuck me, Dracon. Knot inside me, make me scream. Give me everything you have."

"Princess, I'll make your dreams come true." Then I shove my cock into her without pause. I stretch her, force myself down to the hilt. She's moaning, her back arching, breasts sticking out, while I grunt from how fucking tight she is. How well she embraces my cock. My body throbs, and I stay there on top of her, hands on either side of her, holding myself as I plow into her.

I give her what we both need tonight...a distraction to forget the fucked-up day. Driving deeper, the beautiful slapping sounds intensify, her hips bucking to meet each of my thrusts. She bows her spine, her breasts crushed against mine, she cries out as I ruthlessly fuck her.

"Keep making those beautiful sounds. I want to hear how good this feels for you. How much you like my cock inside you. Scream it out and drown out everything else."

Hard breaths join her growing cries as she clings to my body. The bed rocks with our movements, the top smacking into the wall over and over.

It isn't long before my beautiful Eve's body shudders, tightening around me as an orgasm bursts through her. Head back, she's fisting the bed sheets as she screams her pleasure, the sound filling my ears is pure bliss. My deep, guttural moan tangles with hers.

"Fuck, Eve, be a good girl and keep squeezing me with that greedy little cunt of yours."

Writhing beneath me, she's twitching with her climax, but I never pause my thrusts plunging into her drenched core.

Her huge eyes are on me, her breath racing as I build up her arousal once more.

"I'm not ready yet," I explain to her. "I'm so fucking horny that I'm going to make you come at least three more times before I burst in you and flood your pussy with my cum."

Arms trembling, she grips onto me, a grin curling on her lips. "Do it," she whispers, my cock throbbing at her request. "Fuck me until I pass out, please do it."

Her core quivers and I grunt as my pleasure escalates. "That's my sweet angel. There's nothing more beautiful than you begging me for more sex."

With savage thrusts, I work into her, knowing that tonight I'm going to claim her every which way, and tomorrow she's going to be sore when she wakes up. And every time she feels the ache, she'll think of my cock inside her sweet pussy.

"Rise and shine, loverboy," Cassius states loudly just as piercing bright light hits me, somehow managing to blind me even with my eyes shut.

With a groan, I drag a pillow over my face, until it's ripped away from me. "Wake up, Drac, we just received an invitation."

"What invitation?" Blinking open one eye, I stare up at Cassius who's standing over us, and I follow his line of sight to Eve who's cradled up against my side, one leg draped over mine, her arm sprawled across her chest.

Her eyes are open and squinting at Cassius. "What's happening?"

"Well while you two slept in this morning after fucking all night like rabbits and waking up the whole neighborhood, I was awake early enough to receive a special delivered invitation from the Vampire Lord, Marius."

I stiffen. "He came over?"

"No, but his minions delivered this." He lifts a piece of paper the size of a postcard.

Clearing his throat, Cassius reads out, "Dignified Kings of Eden and partners, I request the honor of your presence at our mansion tonight at seven sharp to help us bridge the gap between our families. Signed, The Lord of Night, Marius. And it comes complete with his wax seal. What a wanker with his ancient traditions."

"Let me see that," I say, my muscles already stiff.

"You're not thinking of going? It's a trap," Knox states from the doorway, eyeing a naked Eve, eyebrows pinching together.

"They're definitely not trustworthy," Cassius added. "But why would they set a trap for us?"

"To take Eve," Knox snaps back.

They both have valid points, and after reading the invitation once more, along with their dress code, I turn to Eve who's staring up at me all wide-eyed.

"What do you say?" I ask.

She shrugs at first, then murmurs, "I think right now we could do with more allies than enemies. We should go and see what he really wants."

Lifting my gaze to my men, I say, "You heard her, we're going to a dinner party tonight. And before you ask, Knox, you're coming. No questions."

He grunts and tears out of there, Cassius strolling out of the room after him, calling back over his shoulder, "You better get up then, because it's already three in the afternoon."

CHAPTER THREE

EVE

ccording to the Lords' invitation, there is a strict dress code for this formal dinner party, red or black attire only. Finding something to match those colors in my closet isn't hard really—the Kings had supplied me with more than enough fancy dresses —but finding something that isn't overly revealing?

Well, that is where the trouble comes in.

I grab a flowy and strappy little red number among the sea of fabric and rhinestones, but when I put it on, I realize it has two hidden high slits, one for each leg. And being the voluptuous size that I am, my thighs play more than peekaboo when I walk. So do my breasts, barely contained in the plunging V-neckline and too small cups.

I'm all boobs, hips, and thighs in this thing.

Don't get me wrong—I look sexy as fuck in it, and I've worn less during my shifts at Kat's Kradle. Modesty isn't really my thing, but what I am concerned about is being a vampire snack. Even though I'll be with Dracon, Cassius, and Knox, I'd still like to avoid that as much as I can.

I've met Marius before, and he's not a guy I want to cross. Vampires in general are ruthless, sneaky, blood-thirsty bastards, and I never understood what Demi saw in them.

But then again, she could probably say the same thing about me and the Kings.

I'm about to walk back into the closet to search through the racks again for something else to wear, but, the door clicks open, halting me mid-step.

"Fuck me, Eve." Cassius whistles low in approval, and when I glance over my shoulder, I see him standing there looking devilishly handsome in a fitted black suit and blood-red tie. He's slicked his hair away from his face, with the sides freshly shaved, and his eyes shine a little brighter as they roam over me hungrily. "You look stunning."

"Well, get your eyeful now because I was about to change," I say and start for the closet again.

There's a brush of air against my cheek, and suddenly he's beside me, hand in mine to spin me around toward the bed instead.

"Nuh uh," he says. "There's no way I'm letting you put something else on. This dress is going to show everyone what a smoking-hot vixen you really are. And all ours? Shit."

A blush begins to crawl up my neck at his words and the way he's looking at me—like it's taking all his control not to throw me on the bed, hike up the dress, and plow into me right now.

"Fuck, Eve. If we had more time, I'd—"

"Car's here!" Dracon's booming voice comes from somewhere down the hall. Probably the foyer. "Move your ass, Cassius. I want to make this as short and painless as possible."

Cassius's gaze slides back to mine. Then, he places a light kiss on the back of my hand, like a gentleman would. "You may look stunning in that dress now, but I'm going to have more fun ripping it off you later."

Oh shit. His words send little electric pulses straight to my clit. His dirty mouth shouldn't affect me so much anymore, but it does. Maybe more now than before.

"Come on, let's go before Dracon has an aneurysm." With our joined hands, he guides me out of the room, down the hall, and into the foyer where Dracon and Knox are waiting.

Both look dangerously sexy in their formal wear. Dracon didn't even bother with a suit jacket, going more causal with his black dress shirt open at the throat and the sleeves folded up to his elbows, revealing his thick forearms. They are the subtlest details, but they make my heart race even more.

"I'm not sure wearing that dress will be a wise idea for tonight," Dracon starts, but I notice the way his tongue glides over his bottom lips when he looks at me. "We don't want to bring attention to Eve. Especially not in a house full of hungry vampires."

"That was my thought, too. I'll go change—" I try to

spin on my heel, but again, Cassius's hands are on me, stopping me.

"What Dracon is *trying* to say is that he doesn't like sharing. And he's afraid Marius will want to share," he says.

"I don't want to have to rip anyone's heads off tonight," he replies.

"The big bad Drac *not* want to rip heads off? Are you feeling okay?"

A warning growl rumbles in his throat. "I want this to go as smoothly as possible."

For Eve.

He doesn't say it. He doesn't have to. His reasons hang silently in the air between us. He wants tonight to be easy, less bloody, because he doesn't want to put me through anything else.

It's sweet, and so damn considerate, tears prickle the corners of my eyes. I hold them back, though. Don't need to fuck up my makeup.

"But even Drac can admit our girl looks fucking sinful in this dress," Cassius goes on, to which Drac nods, then glances past him, to where Knox hovers. He resembles a phantom in his black-on-black slim-fitted suit, but his long dark hair has been tied back away from his face, making his eyes spark like burning amber. I still see the struggle in his eyes—like he wants to fuck me *and* slit my throat—and I don't know why but that has my stomach flipping with excitement, too.

Man, I'm fucked up.

"What do you think, Knox?" Cassius calls to him,

teasing. "Makes you wanna…" he thrusts the air a few times for emphasis, "again, right?"

Knox's eyes only narrow on him in warning.

"Come on, don't be shy. I thought we were past all that."

"Leave him alone, Cassius," I say, touching his arm.

Dracon glances at his cell phone. "We're wasting time. Besides, our driver is waiting."

"Fine." Cassius throws me a wink. "That just means I don't have to share later."

Holding up his hand to the scanner, the elevator dings and the doors roll open. We file in and the cart starts to descend.

When we step out, a large black SUV with tinted windows and shiny silver rims waits for us. Dracon holds the door for me, while Cassius helps me in, and it takes me a second to realize how normal this is all starting to feel. Not too long ago, I'd been taken by these monstrous men. Held against my will. And now they are complimenting me, holding doors, and helping me not trip in my high heels. It's bizarre.

But we have been through a lot in such a short amount of time—things normal people have nightmares about—and it wasn't going to get easier anytime soon.

I needed them, as much as I hate to admit it. It's more than that. I…want them with me.

I couldn't imagine facing tomorrow, let alone tonight, with anyone else.

Boy, had things changed.

I settle into the plush backseat of the SUV, feeling

the cool leather through the thin material of the dress. Knox slides in next to me, his knees hitting the back of the middle row. It's clear he's uncomfortable, but he doesn't seem fazed by the lack of room.

"Why don't you sit up front?" I ask him. "I can sit back here by myself."

"I'm fine," he mutters.

"He's worried about you," Cassius chuckles as he and Dracon take their places in the middle row. "I think it's sweet."

Dracon rolls his eyes and adjusts himself in the cramped space. These three men are massive. It's no wonder we took a limousine when we went to the charity auction.

But then…why weren't we taking it now?

"Are we all ready to roll?"

The familiar female's voice has my gaze snapping to the rearview mirror, where—to my complete surprise—Taliah's big brown eyes are staring back at me. She spins in her seat, smiling broadly.

"Taliah!" I squeal and try to lean in between Dracon's and Cassius's massive shoulders. "You're driving us?"

She opens her mouth to respond, but Dracon answers first. "I gave her a promotion of sorts, to help her pay off some of her debts. And after our little issues with our last driver—"

Cassius snorts. "Dude was slower than a turtle in mud."

"—we needed the job to go to someone we could trust," Dracon finishes, without missing a beat.

"What a compliment," Taliah says. Her entire face brightens. "Thank you."

"It helps that you have a lead foot too," Cassius quips with a chuckle.

"Whatever, I'll take it." She turns back in her seat and meets my eyes again in the mirror. "Now, all buckled in?"

Dracon snorts. "Just drive."

"Right." Taliah's shoulders tense, but she reaches for the screen on the dashboard and hits "Start." By the ETA on the navigation map, it looks like the vampire's territory is on the other side of Andover City. She hits the gas, the SUV lurching forward and making us all jerk in our seats. "Oops. Still getting used to the power in this one." But then she easily drives out of the garage and into the dark street.

As we make our way through the traffic and normal city construction, Cassius and Dracon chat to each other in hushed tones about their plans tonight if something goes south with Marius and the vampires. I try to tune it out because thinking about the last time Marius and the Lords showed up at the Tower makes my stomach clench with anxiety.

When a sharp snapping sound comes from beside me, I turn to find Knox playing with a rubber band on his wrist, stretching it tight and releasing, so that it snaps against his pale skin. Over and over, a red mark quickly forming.

I want to ask him why he's doing it—it looks painful —but I know better than to question Knox's *quirks*.

Besides, he's been off ever since he lost his blade. Like a part of him is missing and it's throwing him off-kilter.

It's better if I don't ask.

"Eve." His voice skitters across my skin, so low I'm not even sure he's said anything out loud. But I *feel* the words.

"Yes…" I hiss out on an exhale. I don't know how he's able to do that, affect me so much without doing much at all. Without even trying.

He takes my hand and I hold my breath. His touch is stiff, awkward, but so gentle, it throws me for a loop. It makes me think about what Cassius said about him being worried about me, and that being why he wanted to sit by me.

"Is something wrong?" I ask him softly.

He doesn't respond. Only pulls the rubber band off his wrist and loops it around mine, like a bracelet.

"What's this for?"

Chin lifting, he stares at me for a moment, saying nothing as his gaze roams over my face. I wait.

"Protection," he responds finally.

With a rubber band? "I—I don't understand."

"When you're in a dangerous situation, faced with death, you need to use whatever you can to survive," he says, expression stone cold.

"You mean, faced with you," I half-joke to try and break the tension, but his face never changes.

"Yes. Aris won't take it easy on you just because you're his daughter. Vampires won't stop feeding when the hunger takes over. You need to fight. Make it hard for them until you find your window to escape."

His words are ominous. My skin crawls.

I don't know what damage I could do with a rubber band, but if Knox thinks I need it, it has to be for a good reason. He is the master of death after all.

"I did pop out Franco's eye with my heel." I lean to the side to show him the stilettos I'm wearing. "I can always do that again."

That makes a smile flirt with his lips. "Whatever it takes. With the three of us around, you'll be protected, but when it comes to Aris…and without my blade…" He pauses and straightens. "Just stay close to us. At all times."

I swallow hard and nod. "Right."

Glancing at the navigation screen on the dashboard, I realize we're almost at our destination, and my anxiousness kicks up a notch. As I peer out the darkened window, I see we're passing a lot of abandoned textile factories—big brick structures with broken windows and graffitied walls. When we turn into what looks to be an underground parking garage, I sit up a little straighter.

This can't be the Lord's safe house, their nest. It's too out in the open.

But then again, the Tower isn't really hidden either. Something about ego and not being afraid of anyone else, I'm assuming.

Taliah stops the SUV in the middle of the empty space. "Where am I supposed to go?" she asks.

"I'm assuming down," Cassius says. "We know going up leads nowhere."

Taliah nods and swings us toward the down ramp.

As we drive through the empty parking garage, the car hums loudly, the sounds amplified. Dracon winces, sticking his finger in his ear and wiggling it about, and my only guess is that his advanced shifter hearing doesn't like the echoes in here, more than the rest of us.

I can't shake off the feeling of unease that settles deep in my gut. The place looks abandoned and lifeless, and the temperature drops as we descend deeper into the lower levels.

When we finally reach the bottom, I see a set of massive metal doors ahead, and my anxiety spikes as I notice the cameras hanging from the corners, all trained on our car.

Looking out his own window, Knox notices them too. "They have eyes on us," he says. "Do you want me to take them out?"

"We don't want to kill anyone yet. We just got here," Cassius teases.

"The cameras," Knox clarifies with an annoyed snort, but Dracon answers with a swift shake of his head.

"Let them watch. It means we're in the right place."

As the doors roll open, a terrible scraping sound rings through the garage, making Dracon curse. We drive inside, and are instantly enveloped in pitch-black darkness. The only light comes from our car's headlights, which barely cut through the thick veil of gloom.

There's a loud crackle of a speaker turning on,

making me squeal and leap closer to Knox, and then a heavily accented voice booms all around us. "Exit your vehicle. The driver must leave promptly how they have come. Come to the doors to meet with your guide."

My heart pounds wildly in my chest.

"It's just theater," Cassius hisses. "Marius has a thing for the show."

I've only met the guy a couple of times, but I definitely got that vibe from him too. That fact doesn't slow my raging pulse though.

"Are you sure you all are going to be okay in there?" Taliah asks, looking at us over her shoulder.

Dracon shrugs, like walking into a lion's den is just a normal Tuesday night for him. And maybe it is.

"Keep the car close and your phone closer," Dracon says. "If I send you an alert, we're on our way to you."

"And we all need to get the fuck out of here. Got it," she says.

"Exactly."

I step out of the car with Dracon, Cassius, and Knox, and we walk to stand in one of the headlight beams. We watch as the metal doors reopen and Taliah backs out into the garage again before they shut tightly behind her, sealing us inside. I reach for the nearest arm—it's Cassius's. I can tell by his cologne and the way his warm breath tickles the side of my face as he leans in.

"Don't worry, gorgeous. You're with the monsters who go bump in the night. This is our domain."

A few seconds of darkness pass before bright lights snap on, revealing the space we're in. We're surrounded by cement walls, but before us are two gigantic ornate Gothic doors with stained glass and twisted metal bat details, like out of a Transylvanian castle, beckoning us forward into the vampire's nest. In an attempt to try to calm my nerves, I fiddle with the rubber band Knox gave me earlier. It's just a small comfort, but it helps. I want to believe that everything will be okay, especially with the men around, but I can't shake off the fear that claws at my mind.

Dracon turns to me, his expression serious. "Eve, listen to me. We have no idea what we're walking into. The Lords of Night are our rivals for a *reason*. Being vampires make them dangerous and slippery fuckers."

"I know. I remember Marius," I say. *And how fucking pushy he was.*

"It's more than that."

"Don't scare her." Cassius presses closer to my side. "It won't help."

"She needs to understand the danger here. We're on their turf now. Underground with limited exits. We need to be smart about this. We get what we need and then get the fuck out."

I nod, trying to hide my building fear. "I understand. Head low. Don't ruffle feathers."

Knox steps forward and nods toward my wrist. "We won't let anything happen to you. We'll protect you with our lives if we have to, but remember what I said before."

I give them a grateful smile, feeling a bit better with their protection.

The door creaks open, revealing a dimly lit foyer with crimson drapes and flickering candlelight. A figure steps forward, shrouded in shadow.

That's when a thrum of excitement pierces through the quiet, making me nearly leap out of my skin.

"Oh my god! Eve!"

I focus in on the woman in front of me, dressed in a short red cocktail dress with a halter top. Tall, with an athletic build, and still wearing her usual ponytail— well, a more elegant version of the "fuck it" version she wore while working at Kat's Kradle.

Sucking in a sharp breath, I blink multiple times. With all this dramatic low lighting, I could be seeing things, right?

But then she surges forward, throwing herself at me, and wraps me in a firm hug.

Nope, not a hallucination. It's really her. Here, in the Lords of Night secret underground compound.

"Shit, Demi?"

"Fuck, we're all going to die," I hear Dracon mumbling behind me with heavy sarcasm, but I ignore him.

When Demi finally releases me, she gives me a long look over, and then her gaze flickers to Dracon, Cassius, and Knox behind me and her smile falters. "You know, Kat told me you got caught up in the Kings somehow… I just didn't think…"

"Not caught up," Dracon starts, puffing out his chest as if her words have offended him in some way. "She's chosen to stay with us."

"Oh. Right." Demi shifts backward, eyeing them and then me. I can see her thoughts clear on her face: *Blink twice if you're being held against your will.* And I almost laugh out loud. A few weeks ago, I would have taken her up on that. But now…

"Dracon's right," I reply with a smile. "They're my dates."

Her expression changes dramatically, shifting to a pleasant hostess. "Well, welcome! Let me show you where we're having dinner tonight. Come, follow me."

When she steps back, we file inside, my vision struggling to catch up with all this darkness.

"Where's Marius?" Dracon asks, annoyance obvious in his tone. "I expected him to be the one to greet us."

"He's in the dining room, right up here." Demi leads us down a hallway lined with an ornate red carpet and large renaissance paintings of half-naked women or men doing various outdoor activities. Stuff museums would display. The air is musty. The decor is Gothic and elegant, with ornate chandeliers hanging from the ceiling and intricate carvings on the walls.

Dracon walks beside me, his hand resting protectively on my back. Cassius is on my other side, and Knox hovers at the rear. They all look like they're on high alert, scanning the halls and doorways for any sign of danger. I feel a bit better now that Demi's here, but worry still churns inside me. It's too hard to completely push off the idea that this all may be a trap.

When we walk through a huge stone archway, the temperature in the room drops another five degrees. Especially when every pair of eyes turn our way.

The space is full of vampires. At least two dozen of them, each dressed up in the required red or black and looking otherworldly and too damn pretty to be real. They're perfection, but their stares glint with danger, with hunger, as they watch us enter, and a shiver shoots down my spine.

Cassius shifts closer, his hand sliding down my arm until it gets to my wrist. There, he pauses, touching the rubber band and glancing at me with a cocked brow.

"Knox," I whisper in answer and he nods, like that explains everything.

"Stay close," he whispers.

As we step further inside, I take in the classic elegance of the room. The walls are draped in rich velvet, and flickering candles cast eerie shadows on the faces of the guests. The long dining table is set with ornate silverware and crystal glasses, and a feast of rare meats and exotic fruits is laid out before us.

"Eve, sit by me," Demi says. When she turns to lead me to the head of the table, I see two little scabbed holes on her neck, and bile climbs up my throat.

Oh my god. They've fed from her.

I mean, I know Demi's always had a thing for vampires, but I didn't know she was tangled in the Lords of Night like *that*. It makes me sick to think of them taking advantage of her and using her for food. Or sex. Or both.

I'm going to have to talk to her. Privately. Somehow.

Just then, Marius strides into the room, looking like the devil himself in his pinstripe black suit with red threaded detail. With his gray-peppered hair and piercing eyes, he's as intimidating now as the first day I met him. He radiates with power and wisdom, with danger, just with his very presence. Like Dracon, but much, *much* more refined.

With Dracon, you can always tell what he's thinking

—you can see his anger instantly. With Marius, you *feel* it. His expression remains carved in stone, and to me, that's even scarier. He's like a cobra—just waiting for his moment to strike with a kill shot.

"Kings," he welcomes with false warmth, arms open wide. "How nice it is to have you here, sharing our home with us. I like to think it's a little overdue, don't you?"

None of the guys answer. Probably better that way, but when Marius's eyes fall to me, my muscles stiffen. I haven't forgotten his spontaneous visit to the Tower, when he had his men attack me and then proposition me to join his gang instead of the Kings.

How Dracon isn't launching himself at Marius right now and ripping his head off is amazing. But by his clenched jaw and flaring nostrils, it's clear he's imagining himself doing just that.

A slow knowing smile teases Marius's lips. "Please, sit."

The other vampires from around the room make their way to the table and take their seats. Marius sits at the head, while Alec—his second that I remember from the charity auction—takes his place on the left. Demi takes the place on his other side and waves for me to sit beside her.

Even though it's too close to Marius for my liking, I pull out the highbacked chair and sit. Dracon, Cassius, and Knox follow suit.

"So much to discuss," Marius says, taking his goblet, full of red wine—at least I hope that's what it is. It's too thin to be blood. "But first, let's eat." He snaps his fingers, and a parade of servants march into the room, all carrying more trays of roasted meats, fresh breads, cheeses, seasoned vegetables, and that's just from what I can see. All the food's placed in front of us, and our glasses are filled with wine.

Everything smells amazing, and despite the nervous twist to my stomach, it tightens with hunger.

I watch as Demi starts pulling food off the serving trays and filling her plate. She doesn't seem to have any concern about it being tampered with, but when I glance over at my men, they're hesitant to touch anything too.

"Go on, Eve." Marius's silky voice slides over me. "Eat."

"I'm not that hungry," I say as politely as possible.

He tilts his glass to me. "Very well."

Time passes, and eventually I decide to nibble on some bread at least. That seems safe. Cassius gave up and dug in about five minutes in, and is on his second helping, while Dracon's been glaring at Marius, barely blinking, since he entered the room. Knox is...*Knox*, and looks bored to tears.

But at least I have Demi. She chats with me like no time has passed at all. We talk about funny moments while working at Kat's Kradle, reliving the happy memories between us, Kat, Mercy, and the other girls. It's hard to think that I may never return to my life before the Kings and Aris entered my life, before Franco tried taking me and I popped his eye with my high heel.

As other people finish their meals and the conversations all around amp up, people start leaving their places and make their way around the room to mingle. Someone starts to play the baby grand piano in the corner of the room, the music swelling against the steady hum of voices.

Eventually, Marius rises, and the servants return to collect the dishes. Dracon and Cassius get up too, I'm assuming to corner him, which leaves me and Demi mostly alone. Knox is a few chairs down, but he's constantly scanning the vampires for any signs of a threat. Full focus and barely breathing.

"Have you heard anything from Mercy?" Demi asks, turning to me fully. "I haven't seen her since Kat's got shut down."

Sorrow grips me. Mercy was our third amigo in our little group. She was the youngest, the shyest, and the most innocent of us, despite being a fae and a natural siren. I'd hate to hear anything bad happening to her.

"Maybe she went back south?" I offer.

"You know she had nothing good waiting for her down there," she replies. "Maybe after all this rogue vampire nonsense goes away, I'll have Marius look for her. Make sure she's okay."

I lower my voice, gaze flicking across the room to where the Vampire Lord, Dracon, and Cassius are deep in conversation. "Why get Marius involved? You know how Mercy felt about vamps."

"I know how *both* of you feel about vamps." She

chuckles. "You guys didn't really keep your thoughts quiet about it."

"Well...they do have a reputation. Especially the Lords of Night."

Her brows knit together. "Look who's talking—Eve Dalton, sleeping with the Kings of Eden, the most dangerous supernaturals on this planet." But her half-serious face quickly switches and she bursts into laughter. "We just love living with danger, don't we?"

I smile. "I blame my mommy issues."

"Daddy issues here."

God, it's good to have her here. I've missed her so fucking much. It's that little piece of normalcy I haven't had in a long time. Even in a room full of vampires.

"Marius isn't that bad, Eve," Demi goes on when her laughter dies down. "Neither is Alec or the others. They're a lot like us, you know."

My gaze lands on the fang marks on her neck again. "Except they like to drink blood."

"Yeah, there's that. But it's not bad if it's done right. It can be quite...*pleasurable*." She wiggles her brows for emphasis.

"I just don't want you to get hurt," I say.

"I know... You were always looking out for us."

It's a hard habit to break, apparently.

"But you don't need to worry about me, Eve. Honestly. I'm happy. So, so happy here. Marius treats me so well. They all do."

It suddenly clicks—what she's said. "Wait, is Marius your...boyfriend?"

A blush rises up her neck. "Sort of. It's…it's complicated. How about you? Dracon? The demon one?" She peeks over at Knox. "*Him?*"

"Uh…" How do I explain that they sort of *all* are mine. "It's complicated." I settle on too.

"Gotcha. Well, no judgment here. As long as you're safe and happy, that's all that matters."

Sure, I miss my old life, but I am happy with the new one that I kinda stumbled into. Or was kidnapped into. Minus the Aris part.

But I guess my father would have come stampeding into my life no matter what. That was inevitable. If I think about it that way, then I'm kind of lucky I have the Kings to protect me and help me through it, aren't I?

"Yes," I breathe out with a smile. "I am."

KNOX

If it was up to me, I'd have ditched the party at the Lords of Night estate and spent the night down in my morgue, torturing some poor sucker. But even then, I would have done a half-assed job, because without my Mortem Blade, I am only half a man. Half a fucking horseman.

Fuck Aris for taking my blade, and fuck him for making things a million times worse.

Seething, my hands curl into fists, fury burning through my chest. I want to punch something so badly that I contemplate leaving the study we were brought to after dinner to go to damage one of their fancy rooms.

Cassius is suddenly at my side, patting my shoulder and breathing heavily.

He raises a thick eyebrow and puts on a fake smile that's all teeth. "Take it down a notch, buddy. You look like you're about to burst into the Hulk. We're not here to fight, so maybe go have a few scotches and chill the hell out. You're drawing attention."

I growl under my breath, sweeping my gaze across the room. Evidently, our invite is simply for socializing and lowering tensions between the Kings and the Lords. I still don't trust the vamps.

But I have to give it to Cassius to point out the obvious. Yep, most of the fanged assholes in the room are staring at me, all dressed in their penguin suits, hair pristinely styled, all talking arrogantly as if we've somehow stepped into the movie *Interview with a Vampire*. Sure, the movie was fiction and romanticized vampires, but I don't get the appeal. To me, they're a bunch of hypocrites because the moment I wave a few drops of blood in front of them, they'd show their real monstrous faces and go all apeshit for a taste.

Tonight, the Lords and their company aren't the enemy. I have to keep reminding myself. So I push a tight grin onto my face, wandering away from the bookshelf in the corner of the room, only to have a waiter yelp at the sight of my smile. He looks scared out of his mind.

He has no idea what real fear is. If I had my blade...I

sigh and grab a glass of scotch from his shaking silver tray and drink it back. There's no burn, just the smooth, malty taste running down my throat, leaving behind a fruity, smokey flavor. Seeing that the waiter's not running away screaming, I take another drink and stroll away, needing something to keep my hands busy.

Dracon and Marius are in deep discussion by the bar, next to two of the Lords in a small group with four young females who are dressed up in sheer, glittery dresses. Each is as pretty as the next, busty and curvy, drooling over the Lords, having just recently arrived as I hadn't seen them at dinner. Were they the Lords' midnight snacks?

Cassius is in conversation with Alec, one of the other Lords, so I turn my attention to my gorgeous girl, Eve, giggling at something Demi just said.

The sight of Eve always leaves me mesmerized, especially tonight in her temptress gown. Red as blood, the fabric embraces her exquisite body from the thin straps over her shoulders to the deep V-neck, revealing enough cleavage to bring war between brothers—if they both thought they had a chance with my beauty. The dress cascades down to her feet which are strapped in stilettos, and with each movement, the material shifts to reveal the two long slits running up the front of each leg, all the way up to the top of her thighs, giving the illusion that she's wearing nothing underneath.

In truth, I've been wondering that myself because if she came with nothing under her dress, fuck me, but I was going to lose it… and she'd leave the party with a blushing red ass. After I fucked her, of course.

I casually step closer to her, forgetting anyone else is in the room. They blur around me while an ache tears in my chest the longer I watch her in conversation with Demi. Every time Eve laughs, her breasts jiggle in her dress and my cock hardens.

All I can picture is me driving up her dress and picturing her shaved pussy, slick with arousal, then spreading those spectacular legs and sliding my huge cock between her folds, fucking her like an animal.

I squeeze my eyes tight, well aware that if I keep this line of thought, I'll have to excuse myself while I head outside to jerk off. Heart pounding, I shove those thoughts aside.

Control your fucking self.

My earlier thought of going out to destroy something might have been a better decision.

When the words "Kat's Kradle" reach me from Eve's sweet lips, my eyes fly open, and I lean into their conversation. Attempting to look less like an eavesdropper, I throw back the rest of my scotch and grab another from the passing waiter. I give him a grimace and he scurries out of there. Good.

With my attention back on the girls, I pretend to check out the hideous artwork of disfigured cows on a hill hanging on the wall. This is why I could never be an appreciator of art. People put crap on canvas and call it a masterpiece.

Tuning my back to Eve, I catch a few bits and pieces.

Enough to work out that Eve would contemplate going back to work at Kat's Kradle if the chaos of our lives ever settled down. It surprises me that she wants to work as a dancer again, stripping for men. I fucking hate the idea. I'd gouge out the eyes of every man who set their gaze on her gorgeous body. They touch her, and I'd break their bones.

No man in their right mind could sit back and watch a girl they were falling for have another man drool over her and do nothing.

Fuck me, but I was falling hard, and that hadn't been my intention. When she first arrived, I'd told myself she was nothing to me and that I should have just killed her and got her out of my head. Except, who am I kidding?

She'd crawled under my skin from the first time I laid eyes on her, captured by Franco in his warehouse. I'd been a lost-cause ever since, even if I refused to admit to myself.

And if she went back to Kat's Kradle to work, would that mean she'd leave us? Hell no, that's not going to happen if I have anything to do with it. I'll tie her up in my room if she forces my hand.

There's the small problem of her still being pissed at me and not fully forgiving me just yet. But I've got time…if we survive, of course.

I stare back up at the cows in the painting when a raspy voice grunts besides me, "She's fucking stunning."

"If you're into cows, all the power to you," I grumble under my breath, glancing over to Alec, Marius's most loyal right hand, eyeing me with a cocked eyebrow. His attention sweeps to the painting, then back over to Eve.

"I'm referring to Eve." He stands there, hair slicked off his face, cheeks with a smattering of red, telling me he's recently fed on blood. His hands are deep in the pockets of his tailored pants as he lifts his chin toward her.

"I'd say you have a better chance with the cow in the painting than you do of getting close to Eve before I ripped you a new one."

He barks a loud laugh and slaps me on the back, which irritates me to no end. I fucking hate this small-talk bullshit and being polite for the sake of it. We all know what we're thinking, so why the fuck should we be pussyfooting around what we want to say?

That's Dracon's specialty. I'm the guy who stays in the shadows and takes out anyone he wants. I am fucking brilliant at it too.

"I'm no threat," Alec states. "I am simply admiring a beauty like I've never seen. She's something special, isn't she?"

I don't answer because I don't want to be here, making small talk with an asshole eyeing my little dove.

Movement at the corner of my eye has me glancing over to Eve who's crossing the room quickly, heading for the hallway. I'm not the only one noticing her, watching every inch of her—the sway of her hips, the movement of her tempting ass beneath the fabric of her dress is tantalizing.

"Well, it's been great," I say, turning to follow her, taking that as my cue to escape.

Alec's hand lands on my shoulder, pausing me. A low growl rumbles over my throat as I glance at him and then at his hand, which he promptly removes.

"I'm curious, what does one have to do to gain the attention of such a girl?"

The hairs on my nape rise. "I'd be very careful about having this conversation. I understand Marius is working to keep things civil between our clans, but don't misinterpret my tolerance for leniency. I see you or anyone so much as touch Eve, and I'll bring the wrath of the world down on them."

Fury moves inside me, and the touch of rage licks the length of my spine. One move, and I won't hold back. I'm not Marius, and I don't give a fuck about keeping peace.

He barks a laugh, hands in the air defensively. "Understood, loud and clear."

"Good." I walk away from him. There's only so long I can indulge assholes, and I'm crossing the room, scanning for Eve before heading out the back of the room.

Dimly lit, the hallway is elaborately decorated to resemble a museum display. Boring as shit painting of old farts, statues of females in flowing gowns, and chandeliers barely providing enough light to see the dark hall. Following the red carpet, I turn left, seeing the other path was a dead end.

That's when I swing back around and spot her at the end of the long hall, and she's not alone.

A ripple of savage anger billows deep inside me at the vamp in a penguin suit holding onto her arm, dragging her farther down the hall.

Fury rages in my veins and I speed up, seeing only red because I don't care who the fucker is—even if it's Marius—I'll fucking butcher him.

In a flash of movement I don't expect from Eve, she swings back around toward the guy, slapping him so hard on the face that it resonates. It pauses him for a second…but apparently that's all the time she needs to reach down, remove one of her stilettos, and drive the heel into his throat.

Fuck me, but my cock pulses at the sight. She's going to destroy me.

The vamp stumbles backward, wrenching the shoe out of his throat and tossing it aside. Blood spurts from his wound, and he lunges for Eve.

Possessiveness rises up my throat and rips me to shreds.

Her eyes enlarge, but I'm there in a heartbeat, snatching the prick by his long, flowing locks and yanking him back. His squeal brings me delight, and I wish I was back in my morgue with access to all my tools. Imagine all the fun I can have with a vamp who'd keep rejuvenating.

Days…*weeks* of fun.

Pressing myself closer to his ear, I hiss, "You dare touch what's mine? What gives you the right?" My teeth bare with a growl, the hunger for revenge puffing in my chest.

"Fuck you," he gurgles as more blood spurts down his shirt from his throat. "You can't kill me in my lord's home or you'll be declaring war."

His response only serves to ignite my rage. "Who said anything about killing you?"

"You okay, little dove?" I lift my gaze to Eve, who's in only one shoe looking slightly stunned. She can take care of herself, but the unprovoked attack startled her, that was clear by her quickened breath, the lack of her sassy comeback.

"I'll survive. This asshole thought I was on the market to be manhandled." She sneers, then wipes a few spots of blood across her cleavage. Seeing this prick's blood on her tits fucking infuriates me.

I knee him in the back, hard enough to hear the crack of bone.

Crying like a baby, he buckles, and I'd really prefer not to get my clothes bloody and have to answer to Dracon. So, when Eve hobbles into the ladies' bathroom, leaving behind one of her shoes, I long to follow her and check on her.

Instead, I glance down at the vamp who's crossed me. Glancing over my shoulder, I notice two of the vamp waiters standing by the door, watching me. Fuckers are gonna go run and report me to their Lord.

"Fucking bastards." They multiply like rats. And as much as I want to rip this asshole's dick off and feed it back to him, I'll miss out on alone time with Eve the longer I waste on him, then I'll have to listen to Dracon's constant whining about ruining relations.

Half tempted to do it so I could stay at home for future events, I go against my better judgment and release the prick.

But looking down at this pathetic vamp, fury rages in my veins. He hisses at me, fangs on display, and he comes at me.

Teeth, claws, speed.

He slams me up against the wall, and I laugh in his face. I knee him in the balls because I'm not above playing dirty, and then grab his arm and snap his wrist, the break of bones loud in the otherwise quiet hallway.

He howls, his eyes widening with shock. "Apparently no one told you that you fuckers don't scare me."

Recoiling from me, he doesn't back off and I'm getting damn irritated. "You're wasting my time." I grab his other arm and bring it across my bent knee, snapping his elbow. "Of course, you'll heal, but it'll still hurt like a bitch, and maybe it'll teach you a lesson to not touch what's not yours."

With a blow to his lower rib cage, I finally slam my fist into his face and he falls flat on his back, writhing and whining.

I feel pathetic that I didn't end this with a kill…

Cracking my neck, I'm embarrassed at my shit handiwork, especially seeing I had a small audience of now four waiters. But without weapons, and a no-kill policy tonight, I leave behind the vamp, having had enough of seeing his face.

I snatch the bloody stiletto off the floor and shove a

hand against the bathroom door, which swings open widely.

I enter and lock the door behind me, gaining Eve's attention as she twists her head in my direction from the sink. She's patting her chest with a damp paper towel. Red carpet spreads across on the floor, bright lights glow at the edges of each full-length mirror. There's even a white couch with fluffy pillows. Feels like I stepped into a bordello. It's only when I glance around do I see there's a door that I guess leads to the toilets.

"That fucking vamp," she grumbles.

I move to the sink next to her and clean the blood from the stiletto I'm still gripping in my hand, then wipe it dry with the towel. "Your stiletto attack was second to none. It made my cock hard to see you drive the heel into the vamp's throat."

She's eyeing me in the mirror's reflection, a wicked grin curling at the edges of her lips.

"I had him, I didn't need your help. Plus, don't think that you helping me absolves you of your stunt with Aris." She eyes me with an expression that contradicts her words. Fierce green eyes pierce into me when I turn toward her.

"I wouldn't expect anything less." I fall to my knees in front of Eve, gaining myself a delicious gasp of surprise from her. Gently, I lift her bare foot to sit on my thigh, running the pads of my fingers gingerly across her skin—I love hearing her breath catch.

She has no idea, none at all, of the impact she has on

me. With my fingers curling around her ankle, I glance up at those perky tits, at her downcast stare appearing more amused than irritated. My cock hardens, and suddenly I'm sliding my hand up the inside of her calf, her skin soft like velvet, and her sweet scent with a hint of her arousal invades me.

With her eyes narrowed on me, she moves to draw her leg away, but I clasp her behind the knee, holding her still.

"I'm not finished."

I reach down and slip the shoe onto her delicate foot, then tie up the buckle around her ankle. The thin fabric of her dress slips down the inside of her thigh, revealing her sexy-as-hell leg all the way up to her hip. Toned and tanned, her skin seemed to glisten.

I hear her quickening breaths, and in my fantasy, I've got my head under her dress, licking up all her delicious juices as she cries for more.

"Why'd you shut the door behind you?" She pulls away from me abruptly and saunters over to the couch, swinging those gorgeous, curvy hips before sliding onto the seat like a panther.

Does she have any idea what she does to me? I have no idea when I let myself go around her, but I'm too far gone to turn back. And I don't want to.

"So we weren't disturbed."

Her laugh is the most delicious sound. "What exactly would you be disturbed from?"

Anticipation pounds in my veins, and I run my hand through my hair, enjoying the way she's looking at me as though she wants to ignore me, but is struggling.

"You, my little dove, are going to show me what's underneath your dress." I stroll toward her, pausing a few steps away, the sight of her naked lingering in my mind, and all I can think about is how much I need her clothes removed.

"Oh, is that so? And what do you think I'm wearing? Get it right, and I'll give you a sneak peek. Get it wrong, and I guess you'll never know." Her grin is intoxicating.

"I want to say nothing because I've already pictured you in my mind dozens of times tonight and how pretty your pussy will look. But then again, that's my wet dream, and knowing you, you'd wear something just to break the fantasy."

"Is that your final answer?" She purrs her question, and I don't miss the push of her hardened nipples against the red fabric of her dress.

My head booms with a heady need.

"Show me!" I demand.

"Wow, you're persistent today." With a lick of her lower lip, she unfolds her legs and begins to spread them. My heart is racing and for the first time in my pathetic life, my purpose is as clear as day.

It's Eve.

She's my purpose.

Sitting back, those long legs wide, knees poking out from the long slits in her skirt, the drape of material remains right in my line of sight.

She's staring at me, daring me, and my mouth twitches with a heavy exhale.

I want my tongue there, to lap up her arousal, to show her how I'd do anything for her. To finally get her to forgive me.

Fast, heaving breaths swallow me, so I get back to my knees in front of my goddess.

"Is this what you want, me on my knees? Will this bring you happiness?"

"Yes," she responds eagerly, her gaze ravenous.

"You're still pissed at me, aren't you?"

"Have you made it up to me completely?"

"Fuck, little dove, I'll do whatever it takes, and if that means groveling down on my knees, then I'm for it. And while I'm down here..." I trail the tips of my fingers delicately up her leg, passing her knee, and moving halfway up her thigh where I pause and make small circles on her tender skin.

She doesn't flinch, but the hardness of her nipples keep pressing the fabric of her dress. Her chest is rising and falling quicker now too, and it's impossible to ignore the fragrance of her sweet pussy in the air.

"Every man in that room was picturing fucking you, but tonight, you're all mine." I'm never one to shy away from taking what I want, but I'll play her games right now. "I want you wrapped around my cock, pleading for more as I fist your hair and ride you."

"You have a wild imagination," she teases, then closes her legs and gets up, leaving me on my knees like a damn puppy. Except, I'm a fucking hellhound and I've just gotten a whiff of my prey.

I move with speed after her, my hand leaning against the door, and I stare down at my doll. Perfect, dark hair cascades over her shoulders, her chest rising and falling quicker.

"Show me..." My mouth is inches from hers, the desperation to taste her, kiss her, is pure torture.

Excitement and a sliver of fear dance in her gaze, and I love seeing her still scared of me. I clench my jaw, propping up an arm against the door over her shoulder.

"Who says you were correct?"

A grin spreads across my lips. "The slight tremble in your voice told me everything. You want me as much as I want you. Don't be shy, little dove. I'll give you the world if you let me, I'll bring you unimaginable pleasures." Heat rises through me, and I adore the way her cheeks blush.

"And you bring death, too," she murmurs, her chin high, but she doesn't catch me off guard.

"Sometimes, but never to you...never again. I will protect you with my life. I just need you to trust me."

I press closer to her, unable to resist, her soft breasts like pillows against my chest, her nipples poking me, demanding I give her what she wants but refuses to ask for.

She starts to laugh, but I've had enough of these games. I lean in and steal a kiss, but once I taste her, I'm obsessed. Every inch of her consumes me, and I'm not giving up until I set things right.

Kissing her sets off fireworks between us. My doll kisses me back with ferocity and hunger, dragging her teeth across my lower lip. Hands on her hips, I grind my cock against her while electricity tears through me.

Gliding a hand down the side of her ribcage, where her waist tapers in, then finding skin at her hip, I swallow with excitement.

A sharp bite comes down on my lower lip, my minx pulling on it, staring up at me with a grin in her eyes. Then she lets me go and slips out from under me.

"I never said you can kiss me," she purrs.

My cock is fucking aching, but I love how playful my kitten is today. Turning to face her, I lick my lip, finding the coppery taste of blood on my tongue. "You play unfair. I'm still waiting for you to hold up your end of the bargain."

Pressing my spine against the door, I study the way she's calculating her next move.

"This is what I know," I murmur, then lick more of the blood from my lip. "If you wanted to leave, you would have done it just then, but instead of tearing out of here, you remained. And that tells me one thing." I reach down and adjust my cock through my pants, the poor guy is suffocating in there.

"Fine, I'll keep my end of the agreement." With a devious grin, she strolls over to the sink and bends over, gripping the basin as she spreads her legs.

I shift a few steps to ensure I'm in direct view of that curvy ass just as she sweeps her dress aside. Here I thought she'd just lift her skirt for a quick peek, but

Eve's going to give me a show...fuck me, but my balls are so tight.

Long, firm legs in heels—my gaze runs up to soft curves on her inner thighs and up to her bikini line. Then I'm staring at her round ass, perched high in the air. But my attention falls on that gorgeous triangular crevice where her pussy is covered by a thin, white thong. Even from my location, it's easy to see the fabric is wet with her arousal.

The impact smacks me off balance, and a growl rolls past my throat.

"Sweet Jesus." I'm moving toward her before she can lower her dress, my fingers curling under the elastic of her panties at her hip.

One tug and they rip, so I let them slide down her other leg.

"You bastard," she snaps, but I grip her hip with one hand and push her forward with my other.

"Uh, uh, I don't think so. You have my balls in a fucking pretzel from how desperate I am to see your adorable pink lips. You wouldn't take that from me and let me keep suffering, would you?"

"I like you suffering. You haven't done enough." There's pleasure in her words...the little dove means every word.

And they strike a chord, punching me in the gut as I already vowed to make it up to her. So, I pull away from her a few steps, lowering my gaze to her exposed pussy. My cock grows harder—if that's even possible.

I'm not a fucking monster all the time.

To my surprise, she doesn't jolt back up but takes her time, letting me see what I'd hungered for, the swollen lips glistening with her desire. I reach down and adjust my dick, my breath caught in my throat.

"Seriously, Knox, you're so hot and cold. Why are you across the room?"

My head does a wobbly spin as I try to keep up with what she wants, because clearly I read the signals wrong. And I'm now one of those guys who has zero idea what a woman wants. But I also don't waste a second and step back toward her, trying to not get confused by her signals.

For guys, it's straightforward. We want to fuck, then that's all we focus on…nothing else comes into play. It's how I've always been, but Eve is different. She means more to me than anyone else has, so I need to get this right. And that means understanding female signals, even if they make no sense at all.

She's grinning at me over her shoulder, so I lower my hand to between her legs. Heat radiates off her core, and when I run the tips of my fingers along the seam of her pussy, she purrs for me.

"Is this what you want, little dove?"

There's an intensity in her gaze as her expression softens from my strokes. Her hips rock and she's presenting that dusky-pink ass for me.

I slide my finger down to her clit, rubbing it, her hips bucking for me, and seeing her that way triggers something in me. I push two fingers into her dripping wet pussy and lean forward, licking her puckering ass.

She releases a raspy, almost choking moan.

"Keep making those sounds, and I'll keep licking you."

She doesn't disappoint and I work on my girl, giving her what she craves, my fingers thrusting in and out of her.

"God yes, fuck me, Knox, please."

"Those are the words I want to hear," I growl, pulling out of her tight hole and unzipping my pants, then pushing them down. My cock jumps out, hard as hell, and I tear off my shirt too, as it's getting in my way.

"When we're alone, I'll be the only god you crave. You'll worship me and I'll reward you with a fucking so hard, you'll dream of me."

"Is that your fuck-me speech?" she purrs over her shoulder, her mocking grin has me slapping her ass loud enough for it to resonate. She wriggles her hips, and I'm mesmerized.

With a smirk, I grab my cock and slide it over her drenched, swollen lips. "You're so beautiful from this view."

She cries out in response, wriggling to get my cock into her, and I fucking adore how hungry she is for my dick. "I'm going to make you writhe under me and I want you to come all over my cock."

Then I unceremoniously shove into her pussy. She groans louder at my ruthlessness, her back arching. She loves it, and I lose all manner of control. Her core squeezes me, and I grip her hips, then slam in and out of her. I can't think of anything but the tightness of her cunt, how she sucks me back in each time I pull out.

There's no pause, just the primal desperation that's been lingering in my balls since I saw her in that red dress.

Gripping the sink, she holds on, her knuckles white and her body rocks back and forth over my thrusting cock.

"Ride me, gorgeous, milk me." Heat rushes to my head, slicing through me with the arousal thumping in my veins. There's nothing like the rush of power when you fuck a gorgeous girl, when she's mewling for you, and working that body of hers. Hell, my pulse sounds like a tornado in my ears.

My cock is slick, fucking her with a vengeance, slamming into her so hard, she's barely catching her panting breaths. We moved back and forth mercilessly.

The thumping in my groin, the throbbing of my heart built up each time I ram into her. Pleasure...I've never felt anything so euphoric and I'm frantic to hold onto the warming sensation curling deep in my gut.

She's bucking against me as she muffles her screams in her throat. She writhes, her pussy constricting the life out of my cock, and I lose myself to being inside her.

"Don't hold back, fucking let it out, shout, yell, let the world know you're being fucked." My cock twitches and spasms hard before my orgasm barrels through me. I shove into her down to the hilt and roar as I start pulsing, flooding her drenched pussy with my cum.

I grunt, floating on the pressure her body brings me

as it tightens. My gorgeous dove shudders under me, sucking in harsh breaths, and I feel like a fucking beast.

"You did so well." I stroke her back, then draw out of her, my cock glistening.

She turns toward me, her chest rising and falling rapidly with hard breaths as she pushes her dress back down from around her waist.

"How are you feeling?" I ask as she hands me a paper towel to clean myself.

"Like we shouldn't have done that here because they'll know what we did the moment we return…"

"But?" I murmur, tossing the paper towel into the trash and pull my pants back up, then tuck my cock inside before zipping him away. "I hear a but."

Her lopsided grin is too adorable. "That was really good, and I needed the release."

"You were incredible." I push closer. We come together, her breasts pressing against my chest, the warmth of her body enveloping me. I stroke her cheek as she gazes up at me with soft eyes. Memories flicker over my mind of the agony in her gaze when she thought I sold her out to Aris. "And a step forward to having you finally forgive me."

I lean down, and she lets me kiss her on the mouth. She kisses me back, her warmth spilling over my body. Lifting a hand, I cup the side of her face as she pulls back, releasing a sweet murmuring sound.

"I'll take it into consideration." Stepping out of my arms, she grins cheekily and ducks into the bathroom section. For those few moments I'm alone, I've come to the conclusion that Eve is made for me. It's more than I want to admit to myself, but all I can think about is kissing her, fucking her, holding her in my arms.

I'm the damn asshole in the Kings gang, and yet, she's found a way to break past my walls. And all I know is that she's mine now…ours. I'll take care of her and no one will hurt her again. Definitely not her demented father.

When she emerges, she's sighing, staring down at her ripped thong.

I bend down and snatch it, bunching it in my hand before tucking it in my pocket. "You don't need underwear. I want you going out there with nothing on so they can smell me on you and those fanged pricks will know you're mine and to keep their distance."

"You owe me a new pair. We better go."

"I'll buy you a whole department store if I get to rip them off and start building my own collection of your thongs."

She giggles, and it's hard not to become smitten with her.

There's no one in the hallway, and we make our way quickly back into the main room.

I see the way everyone in there looks at her as she makes her way to Demi, and the way she lowers her gaze before meeting Dracon's and Cassius's stares, like they know what we just did. Fuck, of course they know. Their glares in my direction say it all, and I don't regret a damn thing.

They'd take her in a heartbeat if they'd been in my position, too.

Grinning back at them, I saunter to the bar, knowing that nothing in that moment could bring me down from my high.

DRACON

The moment Eve passes me in the room, the scent of her arousal strikes me and my cock twitches to life. She's avoiding looking at me and is already with Demi, chatting. But with Knox entering the room shortly after her, wearing a cocky grin and an elated expression of "I've just had sex," I want to strangle him.

Bastard didn't want to come here, so of course he's found any excuse to escape and fuck Eve.

He saunters over to Cassius, whose nostrils flare, his eyes bulging, having the same reaction as me. Not to mention how much I'd love to clock Knox in the balls for pulling that stunt.

"Everything good?" Marius asks, at my side at the speed of wind, drawing my attention away from my men.

The Lord's movements unnerve me because you never know when the vamp's standing behind you. But my agitation comes from Knox, so I shake it off and turn to our host with a grin.

"It's the perfect night and goes a long way toward

building a stronger foundation between us. As tempting as it is, sometimes having another partner to rely on has its rewards. With Franco gone, there'll be a new power rising in the city soon."

Marius nods, not paying attention to my bullshit spiel. He's too busy eyeing Eve who's across the room. "She's really special, you know that I assume."

"More than you know," I reply with a growl in my throat, instinct taking over when another man looks at what's mine like he's undressing her with his mind. It's hard to keep a cool head when I want to tear out Marius's eyes for starting at her like a fucking monster.

"I overheard her conversation with Demi about the horsemen, and that she's in danger." He pauses, licking his lips as he stares at her, then turns his attention to me, fire burning in his gaze. "She's one of them."

It isn't a question, but a statement. Fucker knows, and I should have known such a secret couldn't remain such for long. I lift my chin to Marius and get him to follow me to the bar where we're alone and not in earshot if we keep our voices low.

He pours me a drink. "Have you got it under control?"

I try to ignore the level of fury that rolls off me that I'm talking about this to Marius of all people. A Lord, a dominating ass who would have killed us in the past if he had the chance. But like Eve said, we need more allies than enemies, and that means trusting them.

Against my better judgment, I exhale a long breath,

saying, "We're keeping her protected from her father for now. Once we eliminate him, she'll be safe."

His eyes darken with suspicion. "And you think that *you* can help her against another horseman?"

"Yes," I snap. "She belongs to the Kings and won't die under our watch. Which is why we need to find the asshole before he comes back for her."

The Lord rubs his jaw with his fingertips, glancing over his shoulder at Eve and back at me. "It's not my place to tell you how to do your job, but if she was mine, I'd place her in hiding, then scour the planet until I found the asshole. And we can offer you the service of keeping her hidden."

Fury rumbles in my chest from how desperately he's trying to get his hands on Eve. Maybe coming here wasn't such a bright idea after all.

"We don't need your help, but I appreciate the offer." I know as well as anyone that you don't make deals with the Lords, because they never benefit you. And it irks me how much attention he is giving Eve, how much interest he is showing her. "She's ours, so you need not bother yourself."

I collect the whiskey he's poured me and drink it straight, the heat sliding down my throat. As the saying goes, when you lay down with dogs, you'll wake up with fleas…and as much as I don't trust Marius, he shouldn't underestimate how much of a predator I can become if he crosses me.

Eve and Demi are suddenly at our side. I missed

seeing their approach, too concerned with the beast in front of me trying to sink his claws into Eve.

Fury roars through me and I sweep an arm around her waist, drawing her against me. She glances up at me, her sweet smile all for me, her eyes bright like just seeing me makes her giddy. Fuck, I love it when she stares at me that way.

"We were wondering what you two were talking about all secretly over here," Demi muses, batting her eyes at Marius.

"Dracon was informing me of the danger Eve's in."

I growl at his implication that I came to him with my problem.

"Well, funny thing," Eve murmurs. "We were just talking about the same thing, and Demi had a great suggestion."

Marius pushes a strand of hair behind Demi's ear, his gesture tender but the intensity of his gaze belonging to a controlling man. "And what's that, my lovely?"

"Eve needs to be kept safe, and there's someone who can help deal with a horseman. Vincenzo, the ancient vampire that rules over all vampires."

Marius stiffens, his hand on her shoulder squeezing lightly. "Hush now, it's too dangerous for them to go."

Demi's expression narrows on Marius, her lips thinning, but she doesn't argue with him.

"If Vincenzo can help somehow, we have nothing to lose right now." Eve's voice rose with a sliver of hope and excitement, showing me how much fear she's been holding onto.

I glance up at Marius, meeting his challenging gaze, the tightness of his jaw. My pulse stutters, and I'm curious why he thinks it's too dangerous for us.

"Nothing will scare us," Eve explains, her voice determined. "If there's hope for dealing with Aris, then we should explore it." She's looking at me, one of her thin eyebrows arching, her question hanging in the air between us.

"It's not a good idea," Marius growls.

"Let us be the judge of that," I state to the Lord. "If it's too much for us, then we'll be the ones to face the consequences."

He shakes his head. "Heed my word. It's a foolish idea that will get you killed quicker."

I don't flinch at his snapping voice that draws attention from the rest of the room. "You asked me about the danger Eve was in, so now we're asking for your help. Where do we find Vincenzo? If you're worried about this coming back to you, we won't mention your name."

Marius's lips curl upward, revealing his fangs. It's not often I see him lose his cool. A savage snarl slips past his lips. "Enough!" He jerks toward the rest of the room. "It's time for our guests to leave. The night is over."

With a final warning glare in my direction, he marches out of the room, the other Lords following him out. Suddenly, we're being ushered out of the room and right out the front door by the vampire servants and guards.

There's barely time to say anything before we're all standing outside and the door bangs shut.

"What the hell did you do?" Cassius asks, glancing at me. "Not that I'm complaining, but something pissed him off. For a second there, I was preparing to go demon mode on their vampire asses."

"He refused to tell us where the ancient vampire Vincenzo lived. Apparently, he might be able to help us with our Aris troubles."

"Hell, if all we had to do was piss off Marius to leave the snore-fest party was ask to visit some dusty vamp, I would have done it the moment we arrived."

"I wish I could help more, but Marius has never shared with us where the old guy hides. But he's all-powerful, from what I've heard," Knox adds.

"Then we need to speak with him," Eve insists, and she's blinking quickly, speaking just as fast. "If that asshole Marius won't tell us, we'll find him ourselves."

"Agreed." I collect her hand in mine, glancing at my team, while the night crowds around us. "Let's go home. We have an ancient vamp to track down."

CHAPTER FIVE

CASSIUS

*V*incenzo.

The name rolls off my tongue like poison, bitter and dangerous. When I went through the lists of our supernatural contacts to learn more about him, I found out two things. One, Vincenzo isn't just an old vampire—he's an *old*, old vampire, one of the oldest I've ever heard of. And that means he's powerful. He's close to hitting two thousand years, which makes Marius look like a goddamn newborn baby and the rest of the Lords of Night only glimmers in daddy's eye.

And two, he doesn't live anywhere near Andover City. He's been living like a recluse in an old southern plantation since the late 1800s. So, we had to take a quick plane ride for this special visit.

After we landed, Taliah had a car waiting for us to drive to the plantation. Since Knox refuses to get behind the wheel and Drac hates how I drive (I'm reckless or whatever), he's the one in the driver's seat. Knox is in the rear with Eve, protectively hovering over her like he was at the Lords', and I almost feel bad for the guy. He's not used to feeling anything other than the need for revenge and death, and Eve... Well, it's clear she's awoken new things in him, things that he doesn't understand, things that scare the shit out of him. And, if I'm being honest with myself, she's done the same to me.

Once I was thrown out of Hell, I thought going topside would be a vacation. A fuck fest. I could get my jollies off killing and coming, playing with these little humans to my black heart's content. But then Eve fell into our laps and I can't even think about another woman. I only see her.

Can demons fall in love?

I've asked myself this question too many times since our run-in with the horsemen. I didn't think we were capable of such a thing, but here I am, chasing down vampires in the deep south to save her from her madman of a father.

Oh, and save the universe—there's that too.

And Drac...the big bad Apex shifter is so locked in his head, so determined to get Eve out of this alive, that he's having a hard time thinking about anything else.

When we pull up to the grand old house, with tall columns and a wrap-around porch, I hear Eve gasp behind me. Even though the lawn is overgrown and unkempt, and the old oak trees loom over the property like silent sentinels, the place screams of southern charm and hospitality. It had to be a grand piece of property back in the day. Now, it just looks neglected.

As much as I wish we didn't have to bring Eve into another dangerous situation, I'm glad she's here. She's strong, and she's got our back just as much as we have hers. We're a team now, better together. Plus, I can't deny that having her around makes everything a little bit brighter.

Drac cuts the engine, and we all pile out of the car, stretching our legs and taking in our surroundings.

"Wow," Eve breathes, looking up at the house. "This place is something else."

"It's also the home of a dangerous vampire," Dracon reminds her, his eyes scanning the property for any signs of movement. "Let's not forget that."

"Maybe we'll get lucky and he'll have a thing for warm, southern hospitality, too?"

Not caring for my joke, Dracon steps forward. His nostrils flare as he takes in the surrounding scents, and when he seems satisfied, he nods for us to follow him. "Let's get this over with."

We start towards the house, moving in a tight formation. Staying close to Eve's back, Knox waves his hand and sends out his soul-shadowy things to search the place ahead of us. They zig zag across the ground before disappearing past the double doors.

Eve shivers, making me chuckle.

"It takes a bit to get used to," I tell her.

"I just can't believe they are *souls*," she whispers back. "All this time, I thought they were…I don't know. Shadows or something?"

"I'm just borrowing them," Knox pipes in, having overheard us. He says it matter-of-factly, like it's the most normal thing in the world. "They're able to rest again afterward."

"Well, thank god," I tease. "That makes it completely okay then."

Eve chuckles behind her hand as she tries to hide it from Knox, but he doesn't notice. Or care.

A second later, the shadows appear again, zipping down the steps and along the path to us. When they mesh with Knox's form again, his shoulders roll back. "Vincenzo is in there," he says, voice low. "It's only him."

"I'm waiting for the 'but.'" Dracon stops just before the steps leading to the porch, which causes us all to halt.

Just then, the front doors swing open, revealing a tall, older man with olive skin, a hooked nose, and jet-black hair that falls in waves around his face. His eyes are an icy blue—almost silver—as they lock onto us, and even though he could pass as a thirty-something to an innocent bystander, the age and wisdom weigh heavy in his gaze. Unlike the Lords of Night vampires, Vincenzo is in a long tan robe held together by ropes, like he loved the fashion from his BC years.

"But…" Knox goes on with a nod Vincenzo's way, "he knows we're here. As you can see."

Thanks for the warning. Man, we're already fucking this up.

"I don't appreciate uninvited visitors," Vincenzo says around his fangs. His voice is breathy and twisted with an accent that makes interpreting his words damn near impossible. The best way I can describe it is it's something Mediterranean with a southern twang. I've never heard anything like it before. It's absolutely bizarre. "Or trespassing."

"What do we do, Drac?" I ask in a low whisper. We didn't really have a plan going in, but if he tells us to attack, that's just what we'll do. Without hesitation.

"You can leave," Vincenzo answers for him as he turns and walks further into the house. "Or stay and become dinner. It's up to you."

Ah, shit. Vamps and their super hearing.

Beside me, I hear the snap of Eve's rubber band, the one Knox gave her during the dinner party. I glance over and see her absentmindedly fiddling with the thing.

I can't believe she kept it, but it seems to bring her some kind of comfort, so I don't mind it.

When I peek over at Drac again, his brow is knitted, his jaw muscles tight. I know that look all too well. He's deep in thought, forming a plan on the spot.

"Do you know Marius?" he blurts out suddenly.

It's enough to make Vincenzo stop mid-stride. His head lifts, but he doesn't turn around. "Marius?"

"From the Lords of Night," Dracon goes on carefully. "In Andover City."

Vincenzo whirls around and rushes at Dracon, his hand on his throat faster than I can even comprehend. Dracon is shocked too, sputtering as Vincenzo squeezes, his fangs bared. Dracon's skin begins to twitch and ripple as the power of the shift starts within him.

"Stop!" Eve shouts desperately. "Let him go!"

Vincenzo doesn't even glance at her. "My pathetic son sent you here, for me? With what expectation? He doesn't want to kill me himself?"

Did he just say *son*?

Vincenzo is his creator?

That must be why Marius didn't want us to come. He has some skeletons he's trying to hide.

From the corner of my eye, I see Knox's shadows begin to leak out of his form.

I'm all for violence, but if we go on full-on attack mode, we may never get the information we need. "Marius has nothing to do with us being here. We came on our own."

Vincenzo and Dracon snarl at each other, fangs bared.

The ground beneath our feet begins to shake.

Confused, Vincenzo's gaze drops and then swings over to Eve, who's breathing erratically, chest heaving. Head tilting, he regards her fully, his grip loosening on Dracon enough for him to swipe his hand away.

Eve shifts back and terror widens her eyes. The earth stops rumbling beneath us, but that only seems to peak Vincenzo's curiosity even more.

He takes a quick step toward her, and I step in front of him to block his way.

"That power," he says, his tongue darting over his bottom lip like he can taste it on the air. "What is she?"

"She's ours," I reply. "And that's all you need to know."

Gaze sliding to me, his lip curls up over his right fang and he straightens. "A demon." Then, he glances over his shoulder at Dracon again, whose eyes are blazing with fury. "A shifter and…" He finds Knox, who is glaring at him from between dark strands of his hair, mentally figuring out how he's about to dispatch him.

"And you are like her," Vincenzo says.

Knox's shadows peel away from the ground, lifting in mid-air and hovering there like black tentacles. A warning.

When he speaks, his voice comes out more amplified, like thunder. "I am Death, a rider in the apocalypse."

Shit. Sometimes I forget how fucking terrifying Knox can be, even without his blade.

"A rider in the apocalypse…" Vincenzo mulls over this new information. "Like Aris? War?"

He says that like he knows him, and not a 'knows of him' kind of situation. More like they've met before.

"You know him?" I ask.

Vincenzo snorts. "Unfortunately." His gaze roams over each of us, before sweeping across his property. "Now, put those phantoms away and come inside."

Turning, he walks up the porch steps and enters the house. I look at Dracon, who is rubbing his neck, his shoulders tense and the power of the shift slowly receding from his muscles. He's breathing heavily, and I know he's thinking the same thing I am. I'm not too keen on following this vamp into is home, especially after he just tried to choke out Dracon, but if he's telling the truth and he knows Aris, then we'll have to risk it.

We step into the foyer, and I can't help but take in the grandeur of the house. It's clear that it was once a beautiful home, but now it's just a shell of its former self. The walls are covered in peeling wallpaper and the floors creak under our feet.

"I'm Vincenzo, but I suspect you know that already, since you are here and know of my Marius," he says, turning to face us. "I don't get visitors often."

"Probably because you try to choke them out as a greeting," I say as he leads us deeper into the mansion. Everything is dusty and covered in cobwebs, as if he hasn't touched it in decades, maybe longer. The place reeks of mildew, and when I peer up, I see a long crack in the tall ceiling with water spots staining the plaster.

What in the world... Who lives like this?

Vincenzo raises an eyebrow. "My son and I aren't exactly on speaking terms. I apologize for jumping to conclusions, but you must understand. I like my solitude."

I want to ask why he and Marius seem to have this rift, just out of plain curiosity, but I decide against it.

"You said you know Aris," Dracon interrupts, getting straight to the point. Finally, Vincenzo stops in front of a large doorway and gestures for us to go inside.

The moment we walk in, it's obvious this is the room where he spends most of his time. It's been dusted, for one, and is clean, with elegant antique furniture and working electricity. On one side is a full wall of floor-to-ceiling bookshelves, while on the opposite is a massive unlit stone fireplace with intricate carvings in the mantel. A true showstopping piece.

I can see why he chose this room to make his home. Although, if I had a choice, I'd go with the kitchen myself. Or maybe my bedroom. If Eve was with me, of course.

"Okay, we're here. Now tell us. What do you know about Aris?" Knox asks, his voice impatient.

Vincenzo taps his chin with a long, pointed nail. "You see, what I don't understand is why you are coming to me if Aris is your brother, your kin."

"He isn't," Knox replies hotly, like he always does whenever someone brings up his relation to the psycho. "We don't share blood. We were created, not born."

"Interesting…" Vincenzo ponders this for a moment before walking over to a bookshelf. Running a finger over the leather-bound spines, he pulls out a thick volume and flips through the pages before stopping on one and turning to face us.

"Aris is one of the Four Horsemen of the Apocalypse," he says. "He represents war and chaos. He's been around for centuries, and he's caused destruction every-where he's gone."

"We know that," Dracon says, his voice tight. "We came here for your help with new information, not old."

Vincenzo holds up that pointed nail again. "Patience, shifter. You may be old, but I am still your elder." He thumbs through a couple more pages. "Ah, here we are. 1521. Italy. That's when I saw him."

"1521?" Eve gasps in disbelief.

Vincenzo glances at her. "Yes, darling. And I'm even older than *that*, if you can believe it."

"Damn," she breathes.

Hovering close to the doorway, Knox grinds his teeth.

"I was a member of the king's army at the time," he begins. His gaze grows distant as he relives the memory in his mind. "We were fighting against a neighboring kingdom, and the battle was going badly. Then, out of the sky, a man rode in on a flaming horse. It was like nothing I'd ever seen before. He flew through the sky and landed in the middle of the battlefield. His horse kicked up dust and fire, and every man on the field was wiped out in seconds."

Vincenzo pauses, his eyes distant. "To my luck, I was a vampire then, so the fire only burned me. Severely, but not enough to kill me. And then, a demon came up to me."

Eve glances at me. "Demon?"

"Aris," Vincenzo replies, his eyes locked on hers. "He

stood before me, impressed that I had survived. He said I was strong, and that he could use someone like me in his army."

Dracon growls, his fists clenching. "Army? What army?"

Vincenzo shakes his head. "He was recruiting people to find something. A scythe, he said."

I don't even have to look to know Knox is vibrating where he stands. His anger seems to pulsate throughout the room.

"Knox…" Eve whispers, shifting closer to him. "It's okay. We're going to get your blade back."

"Aris will die," he says under his breath.

"Don't worry, Knox. We're all thinking the same thing," I tell him.

"And you turned him down," Dracon cuts in as an attempt to put the focus back on Vincenzo and his story.

He nods once. "I did."

"And he didn't kill you?" I find that very hard to believe.

"He didn't take my rejection lightly of course, but right when he was about to have his horse trample me, he pulled back. He said that he'd be back when it was time. That I would come willingly or not."

"He has the scythe now," Dracon says.

"*My* scythe," Knox snaps.

Vincenzo pauses as the information sinks in. "I'm not sure what that means. He has Death's scythe?"

"It's the only thing that can kill other horsemen. It can kill *anything*," Eve says.

Suddenly looking paler, Vincenzo closes the book with a sharp flick of his wrist and places it on a nearby side table. "Oh no…"

"That's why we need to find him and stop him," I say. "He wants to control all of existence. He wants chaos over balance."

Vincenzo turns sharply to Eve and makes his way over to her. "And how do you play into all this? You're like him—I can feel the power in your blood. And you made the earth tremble before without moving a muscle."

Eve freezes. "Uh…"

"What are *you*?"

"I'm–I'm…"

"She's not the reason we're here," I jump in. He starts getting too close to her, invading her personal space, and anger begins to boil inside me. I don't like it one bit. Behind me, Dracon growls. "We're here for information on Aris."

"You can't blame me for being a little curious," he replies. "I've never met anyone like her before… Half-human, half…*god.*"

Eve swallows. "G-God?"

"Essentially." Vincenzo shrugs, eyes sparking with intensity. "Whose offspring are you? Are you his?" He tilts his head Knox's way, which draws out a repulsed look from Eve.

"No! No, Absolutely not."

"Then who then?"

I suspect he already knows the answer. He just wants to hear it from her mouth.

A long moment of silence passes, but finally, Eve sighs and says, "Aris. At least that's what he claims."

"Ah, yes. I suspected as much. The War horseman has somehow produced a daughter of chaos."

Rubbing her arms, Eve looks like she's about ready to run the hell out of here. A surge of protectiveness comes over me. Hella-old vampire or not, I'll kill this fucker so fast, he wouldn't even see it coming.

"Eve," he says, his voice low and almost seductive. "You're truly something special. I can feel it in my bones."

"What do you mean?"

He grabs Eve's hand roughly and pricks her finger with his long, sharp nail. She gasps as blood wells up, fear flashes in her eyes, and my demon buzzes under my skin, the rage making him leap to the surface faster.

"What the fuck are you doing?" I snap. "Let go of her."

His grip stays firm, squeezing, watching as the blood bubbles up more. He licks his lips. "You wanted my help with Aris, and this is it. Her blood may be the key."

Eve's eyes widen in horror, and I step forward, ready to intervene. "No way. We're not using her blood for anything."

"There may be something more to your connection with Aris," Vincenzo replies, ignoring me. Gaze still fixed on Eve, his grin grows wicked. "As with vampires, the spawn and creator can always feel when each other are near. The connection is everlasting, and it's in the blood. I think it may be the same for you and Aris. If we can use your blood, we may be able to contact him directly."

"Let her go," Dracon demands and seizes Vincenzo by the shoulder, ready to rip him off her, but he's immovable, matching Dracon's strength.

"I don't think I will," he says.

Wrong answer.

Dracon, Knox, and I move for the vampire at once, but we're stopped abruptly when the walls in the rooms start to shake. Everyone freezes.

The trembling increases. Paintings fall off the walls, glass shatters, books plummet from the shelves. When the ceiling begins to crack and splinter, raining plaster down on us, Vincenzo finally releases Eve and leaps back.

"Eve! Eve!" Dracon shouts as the house sways around us. "Stop!"

Panic streaking her face, she backs up until she bumps into Knox's chest. "I can't! I don't know how to!"

"She's going to bring the house down with us in it!" I say.

Just then, a huge chunk of the ceiling crashes down onto Vincenzo, flattening him in a millisecond. Eve screams.

Even though I doubt it'll actually kill the vampire, I'm sure it hurts like hell. And I'm not about to have one of us be next.

"She's too powerful. Out of control. We need to get out of here," Dracon instructs.

Nodding, Knox wraps his arms around Eve, lifts her off the ground, and rushes out of the room, with me and Dracon close on his heels. With the tremors, I keep tripping over my own feet. I cover my head as more debris rains upon us.

We run out of the mansion as fast as we can, stumbling down the steps of the porch. The explosion of the collapsing house sounds behind us, and it leaves my ears ringing.

When the chaos is over, the earthquake done and the ground settled again, we all turn around to see the destruction. The mansion is in rubble—the walls crumbled and the roof collapsed in. The only thing still standing are the two white columns on the porch.

"What the hell just happened?" Dracon pants. My heartbeat pounds at a frantic rhythm in my ears.

"Eve's power," Knox says, his voice low. "It's getting stronger."

"And more unruly," I add on.

Eve looks at her hand, now streaked with blood from the wound. "I-I didn't mean to do that," she says, her voice trembling. "I...I...don't know..."

"It's okay," I say, putting a hand on her shoulder. "We're going to figure this out. I promise you."

She glances up at me, her green eyes wide with fear, but she nods anyway. Trusting me.

As she slides her hand into mine, I look over to Dracon and Knox. They appear as worried as I feel, but no one says a thing as we all walk down the long driveway to the parked SUV.

We have to regroup, come up with a new plan. But for now, all I can do is hold onto Eve's hand and hope that I didn't just lie to her. That this is one promise that I can actually keep.

"Hey, sweet cheeks, feel like going out?" Cassius rasps from the doorway.

I lift my gaze from the book I'm reading and catch him leaning a shoulder against the open doorway of my bedroom like the hot poster boy from a GQ men's magazine. He's wearing a black button-up shirt with the sleeves rolled up to his elbows and tailored matching pants with shiny shoes. The appealing part isn't what he's wearing, but the way the fabric embraces his muscles, showing off just how big my demon lover is.

Blond hair combed off his face, he's cleaned up and looks sexy as fuck—to the point that my libido might be twisting into a pretzel at the sight. But I'm also aware that with Cassius, anything is possible. He's unpredictable and completely crazy, yet I adore him.

"What do you have in mind?" I ask, closing my romance book, which doesn't hold a flame to the reality of my men.

"It's a surprise. And you may want to get changed."

Glancing down at my sweatpants and tee, I feel rather comfortable. "So, what you're saying is that you'll be embarrassed to be seen with me in public dressed this way?" I mock him and get to my feet, my mind already going through what clothes I have in my wardrobe to wear on a mystery outing.

"If you'd let me choose your clothing, I'd have you in heels and a lace teddy."

"In public?"

"Who said anything about going out in public? We've got to keep a low profile."

Furrowing my brow, I rest my hands on my hips. "Then why are we going out? And where? Is this like a small trip to go out and get some milk and you don't want to do it alone? Because if so, I'm not getting changed."

He chuckles, and god I love the way he sounds, burning me up between my thighs. It's completely unfair the impact he has on me.

"Get changed, gorgeous and meet in front of the elevator in ten." Straightening himself, he blows me a kiss then strolls away from my room, leaving me with weak knees.

I hadn't planned to go out today, but I start digging through my closet for clothes. In the end, I decide on a simple black dress with short sleeves and buttons running down the front, then I slip into a pair of black strappy heels.

Making a quick detour to the bathroom, I comb my

messy hair and apply the world's fastest face of makeup, which consists of a smudge of glittery eyeshadow, mascara, and red lipstick. Stepping back, I glance at myself in the mirror and notice that I look dressier than I intended. Though, the fabric keeps pulling at the buttons across my bust—buttons are the bane of my existence, thanks to being curvy. I tug the material and straighten my dress, then look at myself again.

Perfect.

Without my hair pulled up or wearing jewelry, my dress still passes for daytime wear.

Especially considering Cassius isn't revealing where we're going. And after two days of being stuck in the Tower, I'm starting to get a bad case of cabin fever.

Out in the hallway, I saunter toward the foyer where I see Cassius typing something on his phone before he glances up at my approach.

All his attention falls on my dress—and my breasts more specifically. I flush, which isn't like me, and I glance down to see a slight gap between my buttons. I need to put a tank top underneath so I don't worry about it.

"I'll be right back." I tug at the buttons to straighten the fabric. "Slight wardrobe malfunction."

"Nope, this is perfect." Cassius has his hand around my back just as the elevator doors slide open and he draws me inside with him. "I love the small sneak peeks you'll be giving me."

My breathing is erratic, and I meet his grinning gaze. "Are you going to tell me where we're going?"

"You'll see—I've got it all organized. After the shit-fest with the vamps, I wanted to spoil you." His devious stare slides down my body and back up again.

"Oh, I see." His unrelenting interest makes me feel both exposed and giddy. I'm used to men checking me out, especially when I danced at Kat's Kradle where I graced the stage with barely any clothes.

But there's a difference between strangers admiring, and the man who's grown on you. I crave his attention, and if my dress does it for him, then I'll wear it proudly and tease him.

The elevator opens up in the garage with all the expensive cars that belong to the Kings.

Cassius steps up behind me, his hands on my shoulders, swiveling me away from where most of the cars are parked and instead we approach a huge black SUV with dark windows that might require a step ladder for me to get into it.

Cassius leans against me to open the door, and I feel the erection in his pants against my ass.

I narrow my gaze and glance back at him.

"You like me hard for you, don't you?"

"Well, I'll answer that when you tell me where we're going."

I reach for the door to get up when Cassius lifts me up, and as I slide in, his hand slips to my ass—under my skirt, mind you—as he pushes me into my seat. I flinch at his fingers on my exposed butt cheeks, seeing I'm in a thong.

"It's going to be like that then?" I stare him in the

eyes as he grins at me then shuts the door.

He's in the driver's seat in seconds, getting in with ease. "Why the hell is this SUV so high off the ground?"

"It's the only car that's made for someone like me, so I don't have to crouch down or squeeze into a tin can."

We take off, Cassius not wasting a second, the automatic garage doors opening, and we fly out, the power roaring from the engine's impressive power. I can't even imagine how expensive this SUV is.

My stomach plummets at the speed he drives.

Hard breaths fall from between my lips, filling the car as I frantically tug at the seat belt. Cassius grins and looks over at me. "You okay?"

I nod as he places his large hand on my thigh, his finger inching up the inside of my leg.

"I can ease your tension if you're nervous."

"I bet you'd like that."

"For you, I'd do it," he croaks. "It's not for me."

Bursting out laughing, I push his hand back down my leg. "If you wanted to fuck me, you should have just asked me, rather than pretending we're going out somewhere."

"My sweet angel, I *will* be fucking you today, but not right away. Think you can wait?" The mirth in his voice makes me smile, and I glare at him mockingly when he looks my way.

"We'll see about that. The thing about life is that you don't always get what you want."

"I do," he announces confidently.

Thing is, I'm usually stronger than this and don't

swoon when a guy flirts with me…well, to be fair, I *used* to have more willpower. But since the Kings crashed into my life, I've changed. I once hated them, now I dream about them constantly. My stomach dances with butterflies when I'm near them, and I'm constantly clenching my thighs at the things they say and do. This must be what falling for someone feels like, and I don't want to scare myself, but my feelings for them are growing serious.

Cassius keeps glancing over at me, grinning.

"What are you up to?" I twist in my seat to face him.

"Just thinking that if you can't wait, you can, you know…" He glances down at his lap. "It'll keep you going."

I arch an eyebrow. "You want me to suck your dick while you drive?" I blurt out.

"Trust me, it's every guy's fantasy." He's grinning at me, thinking I'm so desperate for him, that I'll suck him off as he drives us to our mysterious destination.

I burst out laughing. It's not that I don't have the courage to do it, and in truth, my nipples are tightening in arousal. But I'm not one to give in too easily to the Kings because I'm not a pushover. And it's not like he's given me any details of where we're going yet…

Slouching into my seat, I murmur, "Nah, I think I'm good. I can hang out until later." I grin when he adjusts himself in his seat. Blood thumps loudly in my veins because the temptation is there, and damn him because now all I can think about is going down on him.

He's chuckling to himself, while the hunger inside

me for him grows. "It's because I won't tell you where we're going, isn't it?"

"Not at all. I like surprises."

"Girl, you are so transparent. I can smell your arousal but you're too stubborn to admit it."

"Ha, says Mr. Big-Dick Demon."

He's howling now, and damn it but I adore his over-reactions. "You can't stop thinking about my cock and how incredible it'll feel sliding past your lips and touching the back of your throat."

"You know you're just gonna give yourself blue balls," I tease, my core quivering.

I've barely finished saying the words when we're suddenly swerving across the highway, inches from hitting a van. I scream out of pure shock, frantically grabbing the door handle for leverage.

"What the hell?"

Cassius growls, working the steering wheel, giving it a sharp jerk in his direction, when I hear the crushing sound of us hitting someone else.

My heart's thundering and I'm gasping for air, glancing in every mirror I have and out all the windows to find out what's going on.

Then I see it—a black sedan with the back window inched down enough for the barrel of a gun to be sticking out and aimed at us.

"Who the hell is that?" I cry out as Cassius rolls his window down and grabs a pistol from the middle console. Then he's shooting, bullets flying like no one's business.

"Who the fuck knows, but one of our enemies has spotted us and wants to take us out. Hold on." Next thing I know, he swerves the SUV in the other car's direction, right in front of them, tires screeching, and I hear someone else blaring their horns.

In a jiffy, we come to a screeching halt and I'm thrown forward, my seatbelt holding me in place. Then Cassius leaps out the door and he's gone.

What the fuck?

Frantically, I lock the doors just in case, and have one of those moments of complete manic anxiety that I'm trapped and I don't know who's attacking us. My thoughts fly to Aris, except why would he be in a car shooting at us?

I twist around and lean over the driver's seat, hopeful that it will give me a better vantage as I can't see shit.

Cassius darts back, moving like a thundering train, and I scramble to unlock the doors before he jumps back into the driver's seat. He's got blood splattered on his arms—just a few drops but enough to tell me someone died.

"What the heck is going on?"

We're off again, our tires skidding, and I glance back at the black sedan parked at an angle in the far lane, a window smashed and see no movement.

"It's nothing to worry about," Cassius announces, his voice rough and loud, then he cracks his neck. "Fucking pieces of shit, Spades. Seems there might be someone stepping into Franco's shoes after all. Not my problem right now, but I've sent them a clear message not to mess with the Kings."

"You killed them," I state, in as calm a tone as I can manage.

"Slit their throats and carved Kings into one of the assholes' foreheads."

"Okaaaaay." I keep glancing around, feeling vulnerable and like an easy target.

"They started it," he groans, then unleashes a long exhale and settles into his seat. "But that's done and I am not letting anything spoil our day."

"You think it's a good idea for us to be out?" There's a twitch at the corner of my eye, and I'm thinking the last thing we need is for Aris to make a sudden appearance.

God, don't jinx yourself.

"Trust me, once we get there, we'll be fine."

I reach over and wipe a drop of blood from his forearm with a tissue. "I'll take your word for it."

"Gorgeous, I'll protect you."

When he winks at me once more, I grin and settle in my seat too, staring out at the world we're quickly passing by. He's really speeding now, and it's probably for the best.

Once we pull up in front of a large building on a busy street, we drive into an underground parking garage and the door slides shut right behind us. Soon enough, we're out of the car and a valet is taking the SUV. Cassius grabs my hand in his, and we move quickly into an elevator made of mirrors. It lets me see the gaping hole between my buttons from several angles, and I quickly adjust my dress before the doors reopen and two women in skintight dresses barely covering their asses step inside.

Something sharp and bitter curls in my chest at the way they're eyeing Cassius, sticking out their breasts, smiling at him and choosing to stand right next to him.

Fire burns over my nape as they turn to him, the taller one saying, "Are you new to the building? I haven't seen you before." Her words are dripping in sickly sweet honey, and she curls a blonde lock around her finger, her eyes practically fucking him, while her friend checks him out like he's a piece of meat.

Cassius doesn't seem to mind, but as his mouth opens to reply, I answer for him. "He can't speak. A real shame, but he's a beast in bed." I drape myself against his side, and he slides an arm around my back, grinning wickedly down at me.

He nods at the girls, then shrugs at them, all the while they're giving me death glares, eyeing me up and down like I'm not good enough for Cassius.

On the next stop they scramble out, and Cassius has me up against the wall as the doors shut.

"Fuck, I love it when you're jealous. You should have clawed their eyes out for staring at me," he teases.

"You'd like that, wouldn't you? Three girls fighting over you."

His face is against my neck, his tongue licking me. "You have no idea how much I want to fuck you right now. You going all green-eyed over me has me so hard."

I release a guttural groan at how good his mouth feels. His hand slides under my dress, and he runs his fingers over my panties.

My cheeks are aflame when he suddenly tugs down my underwear and crouches in front of me as he pushes them down to my ankles. "Step out of them."

I do, but frantically stare at the floors ascending quickly. "Someone's going to walk in on us."

With my panties in his hand all scrunched up, he stuffs them into his pocket and slams his palm on the stop button. The elevator shudders with a jolt, then he looks at me.

"Now, where were we?"

"You being horny."

"Oh fuck yes, I am." He has his hand back under my skirt, his fingers toying with my drenched lips, sliding between them. "Now, open your legs for me."

I quiver all over at his command, having lost all my inhibitions. Pushing two fingers into me, he claims my mouth and kisses me like the demon he is.

It's hungry and savage, but ridiculously arousing. It's impossible to think of anything but my rushing breaths and how much stretch his two thick fingers bring me. The heat of his body envelops me, the sheer size of him in comparison to me is intimidating. Except, I love my big boys because everything on them is huge.

And whoever said size doesn't matter is kidding themselves. They've just never had a *big* guy before.

Next thing I know, Cassius pulls his fingers out of me, much to my protest, and with his other hand under my ass, he lifts me off my feet. Desperately grabbing hold of his broad shoulders, I wind my legs around his hips as he sticks his moist fingers into his mouth.

"I fucking love the way you taste and smell."

"Then do something about it," I urge him, my body humming and my nerve endings sparking with euphoria. I'm dripping wet by the time he's unzipping his pants. His huge cock pops out and, though I know what to expect, I gasp at the size, at the bulging veins running down the long shaft. It's like a starved animal, the tip engorged and blushing and coated in precum. For a split second, I have a mini freak out that he's not going to fit that inside me.

But the moment the slick heat of his cock rubs over my wet and aching pussy, I moan for more and all my worries dissipate.

"Fuck me, my demon," I purr in his ear, my thoughts only on the flesh of his tip against my entrance, pushing into me.

"That's it, gorgeous, beg for it." He shoves into me, fast and deliciously aggressive.

A moan scrapes the back of my throat as pressure builds within me. Thrusting in and out, Cassius takes me, surging into me with his powerful strength, causing my whole body to shudder.

"I fucking love stretching your little pussy, gorgeous," he growls, his words deep and hungry. Grasping my hips, he works into me, holding me exactly where he needs me.

Staring into his gaze, I lose myself, bouncing up and

down on his cock. Fire engulfs me, and I'm trembling against him as my desire heightens. He pushes and pushes me, a savage grunt in his throat, when my body spills over the edge.

And I lose it.

The orgasm bursts through me.

I scream, but Cassius's mouth is on mine, stealing the sound. He's shuddering against me too, growling. Warmth spills into me as he thrusts into his orgasm, coming hard, conquering me.

I tremble as we both pant for breath. Each time one of the Kings claims me, I feel like they're branding me as theirs—imprinted on my mind to never forget their whispers, their kisses, their sexy-as-hell scents, even down to the way they fuck me like nothing else in the world matters.

We're now staring at each other, our foreheads touching.

"I fucking adore you, Eve. I'm not scared to say it, but I love you and I have for a while. You're the world to me, and I never thought I'd have the kind of happiness you bring to my dark heart. They say demons can't ever find true love and I'm here to prove them all fucking wrong."

I'm not one normally to get super emotional. It's how I deal with crap in life. But Cassius's words melt my heart, and I feel the sting of tears at the corners of my eyes.

"I-I..." My breath catches in my chest. "You love me?" I gasp the words, then I hug him tightly, tears rolling down my cheeks. I can't exactly control them, and the emotions bubbling in my chest are ruling over me. I can blame the high I'm coming down from on my climax, but I know the truth of how I really feel toward him as well.

"Are you okay? I hope I didn't freak you out."

"Oh, no, not at all." I draw back so we are face-to-face, our bodies still locked together. "I'm really giddy and blown away that you actually love me, and I've wanted to hear those words for too long. I guess I always try to be strong and not let anything get to me, but I love you too. God, I can't believe I said that, but I do." My smile feels awkward, my cheeks on fire.

Cassius's lips spread into a broad smile. "You have no idea how much it means to me to hear you say those words."

Heartwarming feelings rush over me like a balmy breeze on a hot summer's night.

Warming. Protective. And satisfying.

Cassius loves me, and I'm giddy, despite having just had sex in a public elevator, where anyone could see us. It's that thought that has me glancing up to the camera in the corner, and my heart freezes.

"Oh, fuck," I mutter, tucking my face down against Cassius's neck. "There are cameras in here. We'll probably get leaked onto YouTube and my face will be all over the place, in a million memes." I'm sucking in raspy breaths, close to hyperventilating.

"Relax, the cameras aren't turned on," Cassius explains as he lifts me off his cock and sets me on my feet. I feel his cum slipping out, but I don't care as I stare at him intensely.

"What do you mean?"

"I know the guy who owns this building, and I told him I didn't want cameras on today while I'm here, since there are lots of people who live in the apartments here and any of them could be tapping into the security footage to see who comes and goes."

I exhale a breath of relief. "Thank god, because I almost had a small stroke. I'm just not ready to deal with my sex-tape being plastered all over the internet."

He has his pants back up and zipped, then he cups my face and kisses me. "I've got you. Told you before, I'll keep you protected."

I blink at this huge bulk of a man who I adore… love…and embrace him. I can feel the pounding of his heart as I press against his chest and there's something soothing about it.

"I love you, Eve. I'm all-consuming, obsessed in love and you're mine."

For those few seconds, we remain pressed together, emotions crashing over me, the doubts in my mind washing away.

We stare at each other, just breathing. Is this really happening? During the most chaotic time of my life?

"I never took you for being a romantic," I murmur, trying to come to terms with it all.

"Then you still have so much more to discover about me. And I'm going to show you." He reaches over and hits the elevator button, then we're moving once more.

He wraps his arm across my back, holding me close to him, his mouth on my neck, kissing me tenderly. His growl is a sexy primal sound that rolls through my veins and only adds to how completely drenched I am. It seems we're at a point where just being next to him sends me into a desperate frenzy of arousal.

All I want is to wrap myself around him and curl up in bed all day, where we talk about our favorite meals and places to visit. Where I can swoon and soften against his body, and appreciate the change in our relationship.

His whispers tickle my ear. "I still can't believe you love me."

My eyes widen. "How could I not when I fall apart every time we're together?"

"You're perfect and everything I want."

The doors ding and slide open, yet Cassius still stares at me like he's seeing me for the first time and admiring the view.

Then we are on the move, exiting the elevator and stepping out into a brightly lit restaurant with perfectly decorated tables with white tablecloths dotting the circular room. The walls around us are all windows, giving the impression we are dining in the clouds.

My mouth drops open at the opulence and beauty of the place, when I notice a young man in a white shirt and fitted black pants smiling at us, bowing low.

"We've been expecting you, this way." He waves for us to follow him, and Cassius waits for me to take the lead, but follows close behind me.

Part of me is buzzing that he's brought me to a restaurant where it appears we're the first guests.

We're taken up three steps to a table with two chairs on a platform that steps out onto a glass floor. My heart's thundering with nerves, with excitement, with awe.

The waiter holds the chair out for me and I take a seat. Cassius sits across from me at a table decorated with a vase of roses. But I'm too occupied staring down through the glass floor below us where the city lingers way down there. My head spins slightly at the dizzying heights.

"My name is Liam, and I will be your waiter for today. Your menu and wines have already been preselected for you, all you have to do is enjoy your meal." With a smile, the waiter walks toward the kitchen.

I stare at Cassius with a huge smile. "This is super fancy. I didn't think you'd frequent a place like this, but I love that you've organized this for us."

He shrugs casually. "Sometimes I enjoy the finer things. Besides, this isn't about me, but you. I want to show you the world, to experience everything with you. And we start at the first restaurant that Dracon brought me to when I joined the Kings. It holds fond memories for me at a time I was lost. And this is where I wanted to tell you how much I love you."

His hand reaches for mine across the table, and everything is still spinning in my mind, but Cassius has always been the one to surprise me.

"So, I guess your intention wasn't to say it in the

elevator when you had me up against the wall?" I laugh softly.

"Nope, but it worked out better this way. I told you we'd have sex today. See, I always keep my word. And it was better than I could have dreamed of. I booked out the whole restaurant, and we have a live band starting soon, so you can just be yourself."

Our gazes lock, and part of me wants to crawl across the table and sit on his lap, which I may just do. "I'll definitely never forget today." I get to my feet, and he does the same, looking perplexed at first.

"Everything okay?"

"I need to go to the bathroom and clean up a bit, then you can continue making me swoon." My cheeks hurt from how much he's got me smiling.

He steps closer to me and pulls something out from his back pocket and hands it to me. "I brought you a new pair of panties, as I knew you'd need them." He winks at me.

I glance at the tag still on the underwear and grin, and I blush. "You completely surprise me."

"I love you," he whispers as I turn away.

"I love you too," I say over my shoulders and hurry to the bathroom, unable to believe how, for once, something amazing is happening to me.

Whatever the future brings, all I care about is this moment. I yearn to let myself get spoiled and adored by Cassius. Most of all, I want to lose myself in his love.

CHAPTER SEVEN

EVE

"*H*e said the L word?" Tahlia whispers, her eyes wide. She shuffles close to me on the couch. "Oh, damn, I knew the guys were head-over-heels smitten for you, so it shouldn't surprise me, but still… Cassius is a player and, you know, being a demon and all, they can sometimes lack the finer emotions."

I smirk, feeling giddy all over talking about my date with Cassius in the city. "Well, that guy is not lacking any emotions. He's exploding with them."

She's staring at me, grinning. "You should see yourself and how happy you look. You wouldn't even think you were about to face the end of the world with the danger on your heels."

Sighing, I nod and groan. "Don't remind me. I want to just float on the high that someone loves me."

"I'm pretty sure all three do."

I scoff and break into a choked laugh. "I want to

believe that so badly, but I'm also aware of how unpredictable they are…especially Knox. Things have always been complicated between us." I think back to Knox and me in the Lords' bathroom, the mind-blowing sex, and him insisting on making it up to me. Maybe there's hope there, but I can't let myself believe in fantasies until they become real. I've been hurt too many times to be blinded by my growing emotions.

That's how people get ruined and broken.

"Anyway," I say, glancing up to ensure none of the guys are eavesdropping on us talking in the living room. "Have we decided on a movie to watch?"

It's not that I'm being lazy by having movie time in the middle of the day, but Dracon was majorly pissed when he found out Cassius had taken me out of the Tower, and now I'm to stay indoors and remain safe while they search for Aris and a way to destroy him. I'm annoyed, so I took the opportunity to spend time with Tahlia and feel semi-normal, talking to another girl.

It did take some convincing on Dracon's part, but seeing as Tahlia works for him, in the end he agreed to us spending some time together. He must have noticed I'm going slowly batshit crazy with boredom because he finally relented.

Tahlia leans over to the coffee table and collects her latte and leans back, smiling. "It's not often I get to rest for a couple of hours. When I have time off, which is rare, I've taken up Ninjutsu training."

"Woah, badass chick. I love it."

She hums amusingly. "Don't celebrate too early. I've been at it for three months, and I'm still at entry level, but I'm nothing if not persistent." She sips her coffee, and I grab mine.

"Maybe if we survive everything coming our way, I'll join you one day. Would be nice to surprise the guys with my moves."

She frowns sympathetically. "You *will* survive." She reaches over, her hand on my arm. "There's no way Aris can come out on top because when he comes for you, the Kings will fight to the end to save you. They'll literally burn down the world if that's what it takes."

"That's what scares me. I don't want them to get hurt. He's coming for me, so I will have to find a way to confront him eventually. I know this, and it terrifies me."

Her face scrunches up with the worry I feel deep inside, and something rolls through my stomach at the imminent danger, knowing the unknown is coming for me.

"Come on, let's put on something funny for us to watch. We need to laugh, even if only for a short time. How does that sound?" With the remote control in hand, she starts flicking through Netflix for something to watch.

At that moment, I really appreciate Tahlia's company more than she knows. There's no judgment in her voice, and she genuinely cares. The way she looks at me…it's like she means every word, and that makes me content.

She selects a romance-comedy, and we settle back, coffee in our hands and a bowl of candy between us.

She glances over at me. "I think you don't give yourself enough credit for how badass you are. Dracon told me about your past and how hard you worked at Kat's Kradle. What Franco had done to you, how you fought him. Girl, most people would completely crumble if that happened to them. But you never gave up, and look where you are now. I don't know all the details of your life, but I've seen enough to know you have the courage to beat the odds. In my eyes, you're incredible because you never let anyone trample on you."

My throat thickens because I've never seen myself as any kind of hero for just surviving. The pain of discovering what Aris had done to my mother, and remembering how much she loathed me still stung my chest.

"It's all I've known most of my life. Fight, or I'll never survive. I can't even say I gained that from my mother, as she was the laziest person you'd ever meet and she detested me." I shrug and take a drink from my coffee, my hands slightly shaking from talking so candidly about myself.

"See, and you've come out of that situation stronger for it. You didn't let it own you. You're amazing, Eve. Never forget that."

I'm blinking away the tears that lately seem to be making more frequent appearances. I lean against her, saying, "Thanks for saying those kind words. It means a lot. And let's do girls' day together more often."

"I'd love that." Settling down, she hits play and we both slouched on the couch, my mind swirling with her words

I've never been someone to back down, and for too long I assumed the world was against me, so I fought back… But maybe Tahlia is right, and I am a badass.

DRACON

*C*reak!

I startle awake, ripped from the fucking nightmare that haunts me, and I open my eyes to the moonlight hue carving through the darkness of my bedroom. Heat smothers me, my hair stuck to my head.

But someone's in my room, and before I move, I draw in a sharp breath, my nostrils flaring.

Honey sweetness.

The faint scent of perspiration.

And the delicious hint of slick that has my cock stirring instantly.

"Are you going to come in or just linger in the doorway?" I ask.

"Can I join you?" The patter of bare feet on the floorboards approaches the side of my bed, and she's standing there. My beautiful Eve, darkness clinging to her, but I see her clearly. She's in a white tee, her nipples pushing against the fabric, and her loose shorts hang low on her hips. Her long blonde hair sits messily over her shoulders. "I'm having trouble sleeping."

She's fucking stunning, and every time I stare at her, my body remembers how she feels beneath me, her crying for more. I also remember the darkness in her eyes, the pain in her voice every time she deals with Aris.

My pulse throbs like it always does when she's near me. I shuffle over in bed and pat the warm spot beside me, trying to concentrate on anything but the reaction my body has to her.

"Thanks." She slides in under the blankets, her soft body finding me quickly and pressing up against my side, her cold feet tucking themselves under my legs. She's got her head resting on my arm.

"What's keeping you up?" I ask. "Are you worried about Aris?"

She nods, and when piercing emerald eyes slide up to mine, they're full of fear.

Hunger.

Confusion.

I can take her anger and hunger—those I can work with, both ending with me balls deep inside her. But fear and confusion are different, and all the reassurance in the world won't alleviate those worries. Especially when they're plaguing me as well.

"I've been stirring most of the night too," I confess. "You woke me from a nightmare that I'm glad to leave behind."

"Oh yeah. About Aris? I keep seeing his face every time I fall asleep, like he's taunting me. But I know it's just my fear." She presses closer to me and I curl my arm around her back, drawing her closer.

Her breasts press to my side—soft and perky. She invades my personal space, and if it was up to me, I'd have her move into my room and share my bed every night. Except, she wants her space.

"Aris has been on my mind, mostly how we'll take him out. But tonight, my past haunts me," I murmur.

"Go on," she urges, settling in against me, her eyes locked on me like she's getting ready to listen to a long story.

"I grew up in a brutal world, one where the weak are killed, and the strong must keep proving themselves. It's been such a damn long time since then, and yet it still haunts my fucking dreams."

"The fighting?" she asks softly.

"All the dead. It's like my dreams remind me of how many I've slayed as a form of torture for me."

Silence swims between us before she says, "I remember seeing snippets of your past when I held onto your enchanted axe. It looked terrifying."

"Ah, my tomahawk axe that you broke," I muse, glancing at her where she's tucking her face against my chest to avoid looking at me.

"I'm sorry, but to be fair, you did kidnap me, and I was defending myself."

Reaching over, I brush the hair off her face because I enjoy when she looks at me. "It was a trophy I collected from one of the last tribes I battled and eliminated. You see, I liked taking prizes from each battle, but nothing compared to the axe. I'd heard it carried power and I wanted it. Of course, after that, I couldn't activate it as I'd killed those who could. But I kept it all those years, thinking one day it'll find its purpose. And then you touched it and revealed its power."

"Which turns out is providing a glimpse back in time for those who touch it. In all honesty, I didn't like what it showed me about my past, so I don't think it's a big loss. Though I do feel bad for breaking it as I know it has sentimental value for you."

"It's the past now." What good is holding onto a past that only haunts me?

"You know, it's kinda a serial killer thing to do—collect trinkets from those you killed." There's mirth in her voice as she studies me for my reaction, goading me.

"Back in ancient times, such a collection was considered heroic because it showed how many of your enemies you destroyed."

"Wow, and now it's a sign that you're a psychopath." She laughs, and not in a mocking way. "I hope you realize I mean no malice when I tease you?"

"I know." I lean closer and kiss her on the brow. "For a long time, I was a sick man who enjoyed death too much. Who craved it, and that's what haunts me today."

"Because you're no longer that way?"

Unable to respond right away, I grin and nod, because sometimes I wonder if I am so different from the warrior I had been so long ago. I now have rules I abide by to feel more civil, but deep down, my Apex beast is still the same savage bastard who craves death and blood.

"Let's talk about something brighter," I suggest, knowing my dreams will do a good enough job of reminding me of my savage past. And I don't exactly want to terrify Eve away from me, when she has her asshole father doing a great job of it already.

Darkness is already on our trail, and I have no idea how it's going to end, but I sure as fuck am not going to waste precious moments with Eve going over who I killed.

"What do you have in mind?" Her voice is velvety sweet, her scent thickening as if her body reacts instantly to her flirtatious mood.

"I'm starting to think your real reason for coming to see me in the middle of the night is to use me as your booty call." My mouth waters for her delicious taste as soon as the words leave me.

"Is that a problem?" she purrs, my balls tightening at the way she pulls herself to her knees at my side, staring down at me. Blonde hair cascades down over her shoulders, grazing her tits, her green eyes glinting in the moonlight. She's so fucking stunning.

"Next time you enter my bed, do it without clothes."

She breathes heavily, her chest rising and falling quickly, while my pulse races, my head full of all the depraved fantasies I crave to have with Eve.

"Take it off," I ask her with a commanding voice, reaching up for her, my hands cupping her breasts over her tank top. I groan at how soft she feels, her nipple pressing against my palm.

She tugs her top up and over her head, her breasts

tumbling free, bouncing from her movements, her dusky-pink nipples pebbled hard. They're so perky, so full. I even adore the blue veins she has running along the sides of them.

"All of it." I push myself up on my elbows, my cock rising to attention as she climbs off the bed.

Sensually, she slips her thumbs into the band of her shorts, holding my gaze the whole time as she gently slides them down her legs.

My hand stretches out for her, my gaze on her sweet pussy, all bare and ready for me. My fingers slide between her drenched folds, and it's impossible to resist. My dick aches for her, and unless I plunge into her soon, I'm going to burst.

I palm my hard flesh, jacking myself off in front of her, all while toying with her clit.

Her moans are beautiful, while she's watching my vigorous pace with my rough strokes. She's chewing on her lower lip, her lips rocking over my fingers, her sounds growing heavier.

"Yes," I rasp. "You like that, don't you, my little princess?"

I stop beating off because it's her I want.

"If I'm your princess, then I get things my way, right?"

I rub her clit, her body humming, and I can't get enough of staring at this naked beauty in front of me.

"What would you like?"

"I want you to go down on me," she admits, her chin

high, and I adore that she's not too shy to speak her mind.

"Then come over here and sit on my face." I shove the blankets aside.

My pulse rushes at her sharp intake of breath, and I memorize every inch of her curvy body, the curve of her neck, the valley that I'll trail with my tongue soon enough between her breasts, all the way down to her glistening lips between her thighs.

She climbs onto the bed, ready to approach me, and my cock is heavy and aching for her. My hands move to her hips and I twist her to look away from me.

"Oh, I see," she purrs. "You want me as a reverse cowgirl on your face." She's not shy about it, and I help her straddle a leg across me. I scoot down the bed just enough to ensure I'm right between her legs, and my view has my cock twitching—her swollen pussy lips, her scent smothering me, and I fucking love it.

"You're my princess," I explain. "And that makes me your king. So bend forward for me and serve your king."

She glances over her shoulder at me. "You're a filthy king, taking your princess to bed with you instead of your queen."

"Let me show you how dirty I can really be."

With an excited groan, she leans forward, landing on all fours over my body, her ass high. I can't wait a moment longer, not with her spread out in front of me. With my hands on her hips, I pull her toward me. I lean forward and lick her pussy, loving how she trembles against me.

Her seductive scent drives me wild, and I suck at her lips, pushing my face against her, wanting her slick all over me.

She's gasping, her hips rocking back and forth, moaning for more.

When her mouth slides over the tip of my cock, I hiss, because my princess knows how to give a blow job. I buck my hips, pushing my cock deeper into her mouth, desperate to deep-throat her. I tongue fuck her, clamping down on her cunt and give her what she's craving.

"That's a good princess. Take me deeper until your eyes blur with tears."

I'll give her a night of orgasms she'll never forget, because tonight I'm flooding her with my cum in every possible hole.

Flicking that tight little bud, I push two fingers into her, thrusting hard.

Her cries flood the room, her mouth taking me deeper, and we fall into the perfect rhythm of sucking each other off, giving and receiving unimaginable pleasure.

Her mouth is stuffed, and I push a third finger into her hole. Fuck, she's beautiful from this view.

"I'm going to take you rough and hard tonight. We need each other tonight."

She's working my cock, sucking fast, and her moans

of approval are all I receive. I smile to myself at how much she's going to scream as I make her stretch.

Taking her slick lips into my mouth, I suck on her and finger her savagely until her legs start quivering.

This is my element. The only thing I want to dream about. Me face deep in her pussy while she's choking on my cock.

CHAPTER EIGHT

EVE

I spent the morning making a casserole because I had to get my mind off all the anxiety. The Kings have been doing amazing at distracting me, but I woke up in a panic that Aris would just pop out of nowhere and kill me.

Footfalls sound in the hallway and I lift my gaze just as Cassius strides into the kitchen with confidence, his sandy hair tousled and falling in messy waves over his forehead. The longer strands on top of his head have a carefree quality to them, while the shaved sides and notches in his eyebrows give him an edgy, rebellious look. His deep-blue eyes, almost black in their intensity, sparkle with a mischievous glint as he takes in the delicious aroma emanating from the kitchen.

There's something particularly sexy about him this morning, and I can't help but feel my heart skip a beat as he walks in. My gaze lingers on the way his tee perfectly follows the contours of his muscles, and my attention lowers to the jeans hanging low on his hips. He's an impossible man to resist.

"Morning, my love." He approaches me, then leans in and steals a kiss that leaves me breathless and curling my toes. How is it fair that his kisses teleport me to a place of complete arousal and bliss? "Now, I need to know what the tempting smell is because it called me from my room."

I cuddle up against Cassius who grins mischievously. "You know what they say," I quip. "When in doubt, just throw everything in a casserole and hope for the best!"

Cassius's laughter fills the kitchen, and I feel warmth spread through my chest at the sound. He moves in closer, reaching over to cup the sides of my face tenderly, and I can't help but swoon at his touch, at the tenderness in his eyes. "Something's upsetting you," he says softly, his blue eyes filling with concern. "What's going on?"

I draw in a deep breath, and the words spill out of me before I can stop them. "I'm worried about Aris turning up any moment to take me, and then there's what Vincenzo said about my blood. It's been eating away at me, and I still can't work out how to defeat Aris." Just voicing my fear has the weight lifting off my shoulders.

Cassius listens intently, his expression unwavering in its support, and I love him for that, and for so many more reasons.

"That bastard is not going to get to you," he murmurs, then kisses me gently. "And you're not going to face him alone. The Kings and I will do everything in our power to protect you from Aris. I'm here for you, always. You can talk to me about anything, and I promise to listen."

Tears sting at the corners of my eyes, and I can't help but be overwhelmed by the depth of Cassius's love. I lean into him, taking comfort in the safety of his embrace and having someone to talk to about it.

"So, what do you make of what Vincenzo said? About my blood being the key to finding Aris? And maybe being able to use it to track him down?" I ask.

Cassius frowns, deep in thought. "It's possible," he says slowly. "If you and Aris truly are connected in that way, then it's likely that your blood could hold some sort of power over him. But we have to be careful. If we can use your blood to find him, then he might also be able to do the same and track you with his until he finds you alone."

I nod, dread from that thought settling in my gut.

Just then, Knox enters the kitchen with his commanding presence, his shoulder-length black hair framing his beautiful face. His chiseled jaw is dusted with the shadow of a beard, making me fixated on the ruggedly handsome man. His hazel eyes are intense and piercing, seeming to see straight through you as he takes in his surroundings.

There's a certain magnetism about him that's impossible to deny. He's dressed in a simple black shirt that hugs his sculpted torso, emphasizing his broad shoulders and chiseled chest. The shirt is tucked into a pair of well-worn jeans that hug his powerful thighs and draw attention to his large package.

He carries an air of undeniable elegance about him, as if he's more comfortable in his own skin than anyone I've ever met. It's something I've grown used to about him, and now I've grown to adore those traits in him.

Knox shoots Cassius a smirk as he checks on the casserole, inhaling the delicious aroma. "Heard what you two were talking about from the living room," he says casually, as if it's no big deal.

Cassius rolls his eyes, playfully indignant. "Don't lie," he blurts. "No way in hell you heard us all the way from the living room. You were out in the hallway, eaves-dropping."

Knox shrugs nonchalantly, the picture of cool confidence. "My hearing is impeccable," he answers with a grin, and I can't help but laugh at their antics. It's a welcome break from my worries.

Cassius elbows Knox playfully, and the two of them engage in a mock scuffle, wrestling each other. I lean against the kitchen counter, amused by them. It's a reminder that even in the midst of darkness, there is still room for light.

"I know someone who might be able to help," Knox murmurs, shoving Cassius aside, his eyes brightening. "There's a warlock down by the docks who knows all sorts of things about blood magic. I've used him a few times. Maybe he could tell us more about your blood."

I hesitate, unsure if I want to go down that path.

Knox places a comforting hand around my waist, clearly sensing my anxiety. "I've used him enough times to trust him," he says, his voice soothing. "And if he shows the slightest sign of hurting you or double-crossing me, I'll hunt him down and skin him. How does that sound?"

I can't even laugh because Knox isn't lying.

"I know," I grumble, "but I still don't feel comfortable with a complete stranger checking my blood. And a warlock, no less."

Cassius approaches us. "Normally, I'm a hell-no kind of guy when it comes to anything Knox suggests, but he took me to him once when I was tracking down monsters killing mercilessly, and the guy was surprisingly accurate about all the information he gave me, including who the monster leader was."

Knox is giving Cassius a death glare, but he doesn't seem to notice and keeps going.

"Sometimes, we have to take risks in order to gain information."

"Since when have you become Mr. Knowledgeable?" Knox grunts.

Cassius laughs and slaps a hand to Knox's shoulder. "I'm always here to teach others my wisdom."

Then they're both glancing my way.

"Well, then I guess I should take both of your advice and go see this warlock," I say reluctantly.

"And I will take care of the casserole," Cassius states, which I read between the lines to mean he's staying behind and going to eat it all.

Knox collects my hand in his and evidently, we're leaving right that moment.

As Knox and I make our way from his car parked by the docks, Dracon remains sitting in the back seat on an international call. He waves for us to go, which is strange considering he insisted on coming with us so there were two of them with me in case anything happened.

The sun is still rising, the sky painted in shades of oranges and pinks, the air crisp and fresh this early in the day. Ahead of us lay the dock where a few small boats bob gently in the water, seagulls circling overhead.

Unease squeezes my gut. "Are you sure about this?" I glance up at Knox, whose only attempt at a disguise are sunglasses, which makes me want to laugh at him.

"There's no harm in finding out if that old vamp was referring to you only being able to contact Aris, or if there's something more with your blood."

"He said *your* blood too," I remind him.

"Well, you see that part makes me think more and more that it's just our horsemen's blood that he's detecting because we're unlike any other being."

I glance out to an old boathouse standing at the end of the dock. It's weathered and worn, with peeling paint and rusted metal accents. But despite its worn appearance, the boathouse has a certain charm to it. Though in saying that, I could never live on the sea, constantly having my home bobbing up and down on the waves.

Stepping carefully over the wooden planks that

creak under our feet, we cross the dock to reach the boathouse, Knox having me go ahead of him, while his hand remains on my waist. The cool breeze blows in from the water, the gentle lapping of the waves against the shore should have calmed my nerves, but they seem to do the opposite.

We make our way toward the old boat that's moored to the dock and climb aboard. The boat is small and cramped, with peeling paint and rusted metal fixtures. All sorts of strange trinkets and baubles adorn the outside walls, the wood creaking with each of our steps. It feels slightly creepy and reminds me of a haunted house.

Knox knocks on the door, and before I have a chance to second-guess this decision, it groans open. Standing in front of us is a man who appears to be in his mid-sixties with long, wispy hair and dressed in a colorful robe. The warlock is an imposing man, with a tall frame and a wild beard. He studies us with a suspicious eye and my unease is now twisting my stomach into a pretzel.

"Hello," he says in a raspy voice, his gaze only on me, eyeing me curiously, then lifts his attention to Knox. "What brings you here? Last time I saw you, we promised to part on amicable terms."

Oh, damn. Knox forgot to mention that part, and I'm narrowing my gaze at him. Though he's not paying any attention to me right now.

Knox shifts uneasily, and I can tell that something is amiss. The warlock's mention of their past sends a chill down my spine, and I feel a knot form in my stomach.

"I know, I know. But we have a pressing matter that we hoped you could help us with. It's not for me or I wouldn't be here. It's for Eve."

The warlock raises an eyebrow, still looking at Knox with a hint of suspicion. "And what sort of help does she need?"

Knox sucks in a deep inhale before launching into an explanation. "It's about Eve's blood. We think there might be something unusual about it, and we were hoping you could perform a small ritual to see if you can detect anything unusual."

The warlock has his sights on me again, and my skin crawls under his dark gaze. Then he nods sagely and steps aside to let us into the boat. As we follow him inside, I can feel the tension between Knox and the warlock. What in the world did Knox do to him?

"I'm doing this for her because I can see vulnerability in her soul, but there's something else that has her linked to you. And I'm curious. But after this you are no longer welcome here, understand?" His voice darkens, and shivers race up my arms at how cold the air suddenly feels.

As much as I'm dying to ask Knox, I keep my mouth shut. I want to get this over with because the awkwardness between us and the warlock is making me itchy.

We step inside, and the inside mirror the outside—colorful, cluttered, and sparse. The warlock leads us to a small table and motions for us to sit.

Shelves around us are lined with old books, jars filled with strange liquids, and boxes overflowing with shells and rocks. Tapestries and paintings cover the walls, and the air is thick with the scent of incense. It's dark and musty, and smells of saltwater and old wood.

"They call me Talon," he mutters in my direction, almost sounding sympathetic as if he senses my discomfort. "Your hand."

Glancing up at Knox, he nods for me to follow Talon's instructions, so I do just that. He extends my index finger and, with a small sharp object he's suddenly holding, he pricks my finger. I cringe and hold back from wincing at the sharp pain. He quickly collects a few drops of my blood into a small wooden bowl. Then he throws in a pinch of different powders from several glass jars on the counter and shelves. I'm mesmerized as nothing he does makes sense to me.

As he stirs the mixture, he begins to mumble incantations under his breath. The contents of the bowl give a faint glow, and the warlock's eyes close as he hums.

Realizing he no longer needs my finger, I pull my stinging hand back and suck on it. Knox's intense gaze is staring so fiercely that one might think he is being jealous of my finger in my mouth.

I nudge him with my knee under the table because it's uncomfortable enough in the boathouse. I'm ready to ring his neck that he brought me here if he has a bad history with the guy.

Glancing back at Talon, I ask impatiently, "What do you see?"

Suddenly, he lifts the bowl to his lips and slurps back the blood cocktail. Bile hits the back of my throat and I stop short of gagging. I'm reminded of the way Vincenzo tasted my blood too, leaving me queasy.

After a few moments, he snaps out of the trance, his eyes opening wide. "Your b-blood," he stutters, his voice hoarse. "It's powerful, unlike anything I've ever tasted before. It's almost as if it's infused with some kind of otherworldly energy."

I stared at him incredulously. "What does that mean?"

The warlock shakes his head. "I'm not sure. It's like your blood has a lingering energy that's unexplainable. I don't detect anything concerning, but I can sense a power within it that I can't explain." He meets my gaze. "What did you say you were again?"

There's a dangerous sound to his voice when he asks me the question.

"I didn't," I answer, every inch of me screaming that this man is a lot more dangerous than he appears.

Knox clears his throat. "Do you sense anything else, aside from her blood being special?" he asks, his voice clipped and agitated.

"Power," he declares. "It's ripe with unimaginable power, the kind if wielded correctly could be unstoppable."

Talon licks his lips, then glances down to the bowl where he runs a finger on the inside and sticks it into his mouth.

"You give me more of her blood, Knox, and I'll consider forgiving your treachery."

"I want to leave," I say instantly, getting up and shifting on my feet, wanting to break Talon's gaze, but it only seems to intensify. I have no idea of this man's true powers, and I have my fair share of enemies, so I say, "Thanks for your help, but we have to go."

The warlock shakes his head slowly, a sly grin spreading across his face. "Oh, no, my dear. I'm afraid you can't leave just yet. Not until I've had a chance to fully read your aura and understand what it's trying to tell me."

A chill races down my spine at his words, and I exchange worried glances with Knox. He is on his feet now, all aggression and readiness to defend me.

"We're leaving," he says firmly, an arm around my back, pushing me toward the door. "You're lucky you're still breathing, old man."

The warlock chuckles, seemingly unperturbed by Knox's hostility. "Ah, I see. You two have a bit of history, don't you? I can sense a deep connection between you. And yet, there's also a tension there, an unresolved conflict that might get you both killed."

"Enough," Knox booms just as the warlock lunges for us. Dracon appears at the door, emitting a deafening dragon roar that pierces my ears and makes me flinch.

The warlock pauses, face paling at the newcomer.

"You dare threaten my family?" Dracon's steps into the room and motions for us to leave.

As we rush out, I hear the explosion of a fight behind

us. I can hardly believe that the warlock was able to take on Dracon.

"What the hell just happened?" I ask, my anger rising. I'm furious that I was put in that situation without knowing what I was getting into.

"Talon is terrified of dragons" We keep moving quickly, and I check over my shoulder to see the houseboat rocking from side to side in the water.

"Who the hell was that guy, Knox?" I ask, keeping my voice low.

Knox's shoulders bunch up. "He was someone I used to know. Someone I trusted until I found out he was kidnapping women and locking them in the basement of his boat."

My disgust grows at the thought of such a heinous act. "Fuck, and you let him live?"

"At the time, he was protected by the Lords, and he never killed or assaulted the women. He pretended they were his wives and used to dress them up. Sick bastard. But Dracon didn't want to unbalance relations, so he forced me to back down. I released the women and promised to slice him from throat to groin if he ever so much as touched another female."

Anger and resentment ripples off him. I can sense the weight of his words settling on me, and I don't know what to say. But then Knox turns to me, his eyes soften slightly.

"I'm sorry you had to get mixed up in all of this, Eve. But I would have killed him if he tried anything."

"It's not like you to hold back."

He runs a hand through his hair. "I've learned to pick my battles with Dracon. And in truth, the guy is worth more alive than dead. I've used his ability enough times now to help."

I let out a sigh. "And he didn't tell me anything new about my blood."

"Actually, he did."

I cut Knox a curious look. "Are you going to explain?"

"Now you know that you carry power strong enough to match even Aris. Between us, we will destroy him." He wraps an arm around my shoulders, drawing me against him, smiling.

"I love your confidence in me," I reply, though I'm not feeling as confident as him.

Dracon approaches us, seemingly unharmed, and I feel a sense of relief. But we're still no closer to finding Aris or figuring out how to safely wield the powers inside me.

CHAPTER NINE

EVE

*W*here's *he going?*

Knox slides out the back door of the Tower, moving like one of his phantoms, slinking through the shadows. I had come down to his morgue to show him the new heels he'd surprise ordered for me. He keeps sending me random gifts as part of making it up to me, and I freaking adored his last present. Black stilettos with gold heels. So I dressed in a mini leather dress to really make emphasize how much I loved them.

So imagine my surprise when I track him downstairs, sneaking out of the Tower.

It leaves me all kinds of curious, not to mention hoping that he's got a lead on Aris.

Of course, I follow him. Even if I'm in my heels, I can't waste time, and in no time, I am rushing out the door using my own security pass.

Night inhales the laneway as I catch a whisper of his shadow turning the corner onto another road. The roar of engines and crunch of tires on asphalt come from the nearby main road. I turn my back to it and hurry after Knox.

Keeping to the shadows, I maintain distance between us, well aware that he'll easily pick up on me trailing him otherwise. I step over a curb and move along the street crowded with small stores, all shut. Faint streetlights flicker overhead.

The wind grabs a piece of paper from the trash and sends it fluttering into the air, while I take short, quick strides, working on making as little sound as possible.

He turns left, and I'm there, then down another street where some of the stores are open.

Glancing up ahead, I realize I've lost sight of Knox.

Fuck.

I step out of the darkness and into the light of a bar, rock music pouring out and thumping in my veins. I glance at the windows, wondering if he's gone inside. Except, it doesn't feel like a Knox thing to do. If he's meeting someone, I doubt he'd do it in a place where you can't hear your own thoughts.

I keep on moving, the darkness rising around me as I sink into its embrace. I pass storefront after storefront, and still see no sign of Knox along the long road. The few cars that pass reveal nothing with their headlights, so I pause and glance over my shoulder. Maybe I'd been too hasty to dismiss the bar.

Sighing, I decide to hurry to the end of the road when I walk right into someone, their chest hard as rock, and I pitch backward in my rebound, my steps stuttering. There's a moment of panic.

With a gasp, I lift my gaze as strong hands grab me by my arms, steading me, and my gaze clashes with narrowing silvery eyes. My heart's hammering from how I almost fell over.

"Why are you following me?" Knox growls. "It's dangerous out here."

"Where are you going?" I counter, lifting my chin and pulling myself out of his grasp.

"I have business to attend to. And you shouldn't be out here, especially alone." The bridge between his eyes creases. "Fuck, Eve, you know better than to pull this shit."

"Hey, back off, because I can take care of myself. And you see my shoes," I point to my stilettos, "I'm very capable of wielding them as a deadly weapon. Besides, if all else fails, I unleash my power."

He gets me by my arm and drags me aside into a shadowy pocket by a closed store. "Yeah, real smart. Use the power that you can't control." His voice darkens, and it pisses me off.

"How about you tell me why you're sneaking out of the Tower. Have you found something on Aris? Or maybe something about our blood controlling him?"

His lips are thin and he's shaking his head. "I'm letting off some steam and heard some of the assholes working for the new Black Spades boss have been moving into our territory, peddling drugs and killing anyone who denies them. So, I'm going to put an end to it before it escalates."

Most likely, Knox is just in the mood to kill and torture someone. But if he's taking out our enemy who's hurting people, I'm not going to stop him.

"Good, I'm coming with you and you can teach me some moves."

A growl rolls from his throat as he runs a hand through his thick, black hair. He's frustrated, but to me, it's impossible to ignore how damn sexy he looks when he does that, looking all broody. That strong jawline, high cheekbones, darkening eyes. God, I want those lips all over me.

"No, you're not joining me," he grumbles, shaking his head. "Fuck, I can't even believe I'm the one disciplining you. See what you've done to me? You've made me responsible and boring."

I laugh at him. "Trust me, you're anything but boring."

"Answer still stands. Remember how you destroyed Vincenzo's place and buried him under the rubble? He might come for revenge for all we know, but you couldn't stop your power."

I lick my lips, my body stiffening because I don't respond well when people tell me I can't do something. "Then teach me how to control it, how to use the power."

He huffs. "Your power is too chaotic. Don't you see, the horsemen want to destroy you."

"Knox," I groan.

But he's taking hold of my arm. "I'm not arguing this with you. They will remove you because to them you're a danger. There can only be four horsemen."

I step away from him, anger bubbling inside me. "Then just show me. You've done it, so why are you being so damn stubborn?"

He doesn't answer right away, but stares at me intensely. "Every horseman has different powers and ways they wield them. I'm not even sure if I can teach you, but… I guess I can try."

"Yes." I jump up on my toes, which only has Knox's gaze lowering to my bouncing breasts.

"You shouldn't do that." He reaches down to adjust his cock, making a sucking sound as he draws in a heavy breath.

Is it bad of me to enjoy seeing him turned on by me?

His gaze trails down my body. "The shoes look good on you. I had them delivered from Milan."

I press myself against him, wanting to thank him properly. "I saw that they're Jimmy Choo. They must have cost you a bit."

"Price doesn't matter when it comes to you. As long as you like them. You do, right?"

"Sometimes, you can really make a girl's heart flutter." I'm impressed by how easily he makes me swoon. "I adore them."

He leans in close, my stomach bursting with butterflies, when the thud of footsteps echoes nearby.

We pause just long enough to glance over our shoulders to the three men rushing us.

Panic slams into me, heart hammering.

And that perfect moment between Knox and I is ripped away.

He swings away from me and charges toward them like a tank, slamming into the trio, taking one right off his feet. One guy slips free and is coming right for me.

I have no clue who the fuck these men are, but they definitely know who we are. He thunders my way, and I duck his swinging fist, pivoting back around. I drive my fist into his lower back. I drive it hard so he feels my knuckles against his spine and it stings like hell.

Whipping around, the back of his hand knocks right into the side of my head. Stars blink behind my eyes and I stumble as I frantically reach down to grab my shoe.

But he's moving too fast and has me by my throat, slamming me up against the wall, stealing all the air from my lungs.

Ramming my fits into his arm, I kick wildly. It's only then that I notice the inked spade tattoo on his inner arm to symbolize he's part of their cartel. Damn assholes are definitely in the area like Knox said.

Thrashing, I fight for air, my lungs burning. I try my best to ignore that voice in my head that tells me to obliterate him with the power that's simmering deep in my gut.

I hate holding it in, hate the way it makes my pulse race and my head spin. And if I release it, then what? I destroy the whole damn city because I can't control it?

Fighting for my life, I dig my fingernails into his

arm. The asshole is smiling, his teeth stained yellow, a scab on his lower lip.

"I'm gonna fuck you up real good," he rasps, lifting a blade to my face, the metal catching the shine of the moon.

Desperation billows in my chest, clenching my throat, forcing the first trickles of power to slip through my body.

KNOX

A blade slashes across my arm, biting into flesh.

I hiss, throwing a fist right into the asshole's face, then kick his legs out from under him. He trips over the curb, falling, the knife thrown halfway across the road. If only I had my Mortem Blade, I'll have them dead in seconds.

But it's not me I am worried about, and kick the second guy in the ribs, seeing he's already writhing on the ground. I lift my gaze to Eve pinned to the window of a storefront by her throat.

I see red at the asshole hurting her.

A roar spills past my lips as fury thunders through my veins.

No one touches Eve—no one goes near her. She belongs to me...to the Kings.

Destruction. Devastation.

That's all I see, all I feel, as I launch myself him and

throw my arm around his throat, wrenching him back off her. I squeeze, suffocating the fucker.

He thrashes against me, releasing my little dove. She tumbles to her feet, frantically gasping for air.

The glint from his blade rushing up toward my face has me snatching his arm with my free hand, keeping it away, while I put him into a sleep hold. It's a sissy move and not my style, but I'm also hyper away when we're in public and there might be cameras around.

"You okay?" I call out to Eve, who's shaking ferociously. The wind licks me with the bite of her power. "Eve, hold it together. Don't you let it out."

Just as she glances up at me with gleaming eyes, a hard punch comes to my back, followed by two more.

My knees collapse and I let the sucker go from my hold and he's sucking in air like a drowning rat.

I swing back around as the hilt of a knife hits me square in the face. The world spins, and I'm stumbling, swinging my fists out.

Sharpness cuts me across my cheeks just as I jolt backward. Shaking my head, I find one of the assholes coming at me. And now I regret coming out here without a single weapon.

Fuck, I miss my Mortem Blade.

The guy's knife slices through the night, aimed at my face once more. I duck at the last second, but so does the prick.

His knife arcs toward me and I raise my arms to cover my face, the blade sinking right into my forearm. I roar, acid-like pain tearing across my arm.

My gut clenches, blood spills down my arm, and the asshole is chuckling.

"You, you piece of shit, are going to die tonight."

Fury slams into me, and I swing my attention to Eve as my skin pricks with her magic.

Two guys against my beauty, their backs to me, and she's shouting something at them, but I can't make it out. My pulse thunders in my ears, and fuck but my arm is screaming with pain.

I swing back around and wrench the blade out of my arm, blood spilling everywhere.

Just then, the asshole who stabbed me punches me right in the solar plexus. Breath explodes from me and I teeter backward and trip over my feet. On my knees, I push through the excruciating ache.

"I'm coming for you, little dove," I grunt, pushing myself back up on my feet.

That's when I see that the dead-man-walking has a gun pointed in my face. "Back on your knees, fucker."

Rage hammers into me, and I've had enough of this bullshit. Acid hits the back of my throat as I tense up.

In that space of a heartbeat, the air changes, thickens, and carries with it unbelievable power. The ground trembles under my feet.

The knob in front of me is thrown across the road with lightning speed by an invisible force, his head bursting. Blood and brains splatter everywhere. And I'm startled, which I shouldn't be.

But what the hell just happened?

I swing back around to Eve.

She's standing there, covered in blood, while the enemy lies dead in a pool of gore at her feet. Her eyes are huge but, on the bright side, she hasn't torn up the city. The magic's tempered.

But I can't take my eyes off her—that pale skin speckled in blood, dark, sinful eyes holding mine. Nipples tight and pressing against her leather dress, her red lips parting with a gasp.

I lick my acrid lips, my gaze lowering to her gorgeous legs in that mini dress, the swell of her breasts, and my cock's growing hard.

She's staring at me, slightly alarmed, yet grinning. She enjoyed dishing out punishment.

"That's my girl. You did incredible," I coo, making my way toward her. All while a manic, hungry savagery climbs through me. My hands shake with eagerness to rip those clothes off her.

My spine bows forward as I reach for her and she steps over the spreading river of red across the sidewalk.

"I-I controlled it, I think. I don't know, but something felt incredible and terrifying at the same time."

Free of the dead mess, I grab her in my arms and pin her to the brick wall between two stores. Darkness crowds around us.

"You were fucking incredible," I murmur, kissing her, my hand sliding under her dress where I rip her thong off without pause.

"Knox," she gasps, yet goes back to kissing me,

curling a leg around the back of mine, her scent intoxicating and thick.

"You have no idea how damn sexy you look covered in the blood of the enemy you destroyed."

She's yanking at my shirt as I tug up her tight skirt, and she excitedly moves on to tug at my belt and unzip my jeans. With my cock out, I lift her easily into my arms, her back to the wall.

"Hug me with those sexy legs. I want to fuck you, to make you scream my name."

"Please, yes please." Her pleading is beautiful, and I have my dick rock-hard, my balls aching for release. A blush creeps across her cheeks.

"Nothing to be shy about."

"It's just that I'm so horny and it feels wrong."

I shake my head, loving that after a surge of power and a fight, she's horny. That's me all the time. "It's the best time to fuck and celebrate. I also find it can help tame my power."

She's smiling, leaning closer to kiss me, and I thrust inside her. Her moans are hypnotic. I hold onto her hips and plunge into her, pushing my tongue into her mouth. I want the last thing she remembers of tonight to be me bringing her the most breathtaking orgasm.

Her body's bucking against me, desperate for me.

"That's my girl. I'm going to coat your tight pussy with my seed." Then I rut her hard, pounding all the way to my hilt, desperate to flood her with my cum.

At the corner of my eyes, I see the lifeless bodies of the men she killed, and maybe I should care more that we're fucking right next to dead men for her sake. For me, I couldn't give a shit.

Instead, I fuck my beauty and pepper her face with kisses, showing her how much she means to me. How I'm rewarding her for showing potential in controlling her power.

I'm all about positive reinforcement.

I'm standing on the top floor pool deck of the Tower, staring out at the cityscape below. The sun is setting, casting a beautiful orange and pink glow over the buildings. I feel Cassius's and Knox's presence behind me as they set up for our practice exercises.

My stomach twists with nerves. I don't know how I'm going to do this—control my power and use it as a weapon against Aris. I still can't believe I even *have* power, or that an apocalypse horseman is my father. Now I'm expected to figure out how to manipulate chaos and take War down?

Seems impossible.

My men are determined though. They believe I can do it, even Knox, and he should know, right? For some reason, his confidence in me means more than the others. It's probably because I know he'd never lie to me to save my feelings. Or because he knows Aris better than any of us. Either way, I'm thankful he's here to guide me through this. Cassius too. I need his humor to ease my nerves.

"Okay, little dove, we're going to start with something simple," Knox says, and points to the line of lounge chairs on the other side of the pool. "We want you to try and hit that pool chair over there."

"That's like…twenty yards away," I reply.

"We're starting small."

"Small?" I squeak and glance at Cassius. "He thinks hitting something at twenty yards is small?"

Cassius chuckles. "You can do it, gorgeous. Just listen to Knox, focus, and picture Aris sitting on one of those chairs. Blast his ass back to kingdom come."

"Sure, easy," I say sarcastically. I'm snapping the rubber band around my wrist again, trying to focus on the sharp sting it gives me instead of the worry gnawing at my insides.

Warm hands slide down my arms, a familiar hardness pressing into my back. When Knox's hands wrap around my wrists, stopping my plucking, I feel his breath on the side of my face. "Relax." His deep voice is a soothing whisper against my skin. "I'll help you through all of it."

"But what if I'm not strong enough to take him on? What if—"

"Shhh, doubt is a burden," he says. "You will get this. And we will defeat Aris. Now, hold your hands out. Like this." He uses his hold on me to lift my arms and guide them to the right angle. "Using your hands isn't necessary—your power seems to explode out from your very core—but I think it'll help you better focus that power if you channel it through something, like your hands."

I can see the middle pool chair between my two hands, and I lock my gaze on it.

"Aim at your intended target," he instructs, "and when you're ready, unleash your power."

I pause. "What does that mean? Unleash it?"

"Just let it go," Cassius says.

"It's not that easy. It comes out whenever it feels like it. It's like it has a mind of its own."

"It seems to trigger whenever you're under extreme distress," Knox clarifies.

"Like her own personal defense mechanism," Cassius says.

Knox nods.

"But I don't want to have to be attacked to be able to use it," I tell them. "That doesn't seem helpful."

"And you won't have to," he explains. "That's only when it's the easiest to access it for you. It's your body forcing you to remove the wall you've put up between you and your chaos power in order to save yourself in that moment."

"A wall?"

"At some point in your life, you built a barrier between your human soul and your celestial energy."

"It makes sense. It's a survival tactic," Cassius adds.

"Exactly. And that wall only comes down when you're in extreme danger. To protect you."

"Like with Vincenzo," I say. "Or Franco."

"Or Aris, yes, exactly," Knox replies. "So, what we need to do is let your body know it's okay to tear down that wall and let those two sides of you merge. It'll only make you stronger in the end."

"What if I can't handle that much power? Will I just…explode?" I ask.

Cassius's laughter booms, but when I throw him a sharp glare, he cuts it off abruptly.

When I feel Knox step back, his comforting touch gone, I glance over my shoulder to see him standing there, expression stone cold.

I whirl on him. "Knox? I won't explode, will I?"

He doesn't answer, and my pulse ticks up.

"Come on, Knox. Let's not torture the girl." Cassius's voice is tinged with laughter but it's quickly dying as he sees the seriousness on Knox's face. "Tell her that's not true."

His gaze flicks between us.

"Knox!" I yelp.

He sighs. "Explode, no. I don't believe that is what'll happen. Although the fact that you're still alive after tapping into that side of yourself is a good sign, there's no way to know for sure what'll happen once the flood-gates are opened fully. It may be too much…" His words fade away, but I hear the unspoken part loud and clear in my head.

It could kill me.

Fear grips me. "Why didn't you tell me this before?" I shout, frantic.

"Yeah, Knox. That's a bit of useful information,

something you share," Cassius says. "Does Dracon know this?"

He shakes his head. "But it doesn't matter. If she doesn't at least try, then Aris wins, and we're all dead anyway. With the Mortem Blade, he's unstoppable."

Fuck. I can't believe this is happening right now.

"This was only supposed to be a simple practice session, Knox! Not life or death!" Cassius pushes fingers through his hair over and over as he begins to pace. For him, the risk to me is too great, and his compassion for me touches me deep.

He changes direction and heads for the door. "I'm going to tell Dracon. He'll want to know. Then he can tell us what to do next."

"Wait," I call out.

Cassius pauses.

Closing my eyes, I draw in a deep breath. I can't believe I'm about to say this, but... "Knox is right. It doesn't matter."

Cassius closes the distance between us in a flash, palm pressing against my cheek and staring down at me with those electrifying eyes. "Eve, I swear to god, if you tell me it's because you don't matter or you're not good enough, I'll–I'll–"

The demon flashes over his handsome face, and the intensity of what he's saying sinks me. When I was young, I always felt like I wasn't good enough. For my mother, my friends, my father...sometimes, even myself. It took me a long time to like myself and not get stuck in the sting of rejection or cycle of self-doubt.

I have three otherworldly men who would burn down the world for me, risk their lives for me, do anything for me. I shouldn't be questioning myself now.

Sure, the idea of facing Aris is scary as fuck, but I can't get caught up in that fear. Knox is right. I've come this far. I've survived that celestial part of me already, and I can handle more. I know I can.

I press my hand against Cassius's. "It doesn't matter because I know what I have to do," I assure him. "The power won't hurt me. It's part of me. I just need to learn how to channel it better. And that's why you're here." I turn to Knox. "And you."

Knox's lips lift in a small smile. "That's right, little dove, and I'll help you every step of the way."

Cassius's hand falls away with a defeated sigh. "Fine. If you're sure you're okay with this."

"I am." I give a stiff nod, and turn to take my position again, facing the line of chairs. Cassius comes to my right with Knox on my left.

"When you're ready, little dove, hands up, aim at the chair you want to hit, and allow that inner wall to come down. Let the power flow through you, flow out of you, and through your fingers."

Not sure how to do that *exactly*, I move my hands into the right position, take a deep breath to relax myself, and start to talk to myself inwardly.

You aren't weak, Eve. All your life, people have underestimated you because of your size, your parentage, your job... But you've risen above it all. You're the one who decides the life you want to live. You. Not your mother. Not Aris.

You control this power. It doesn't control you.

I focus my thoughts on the chair, trying to shoot a blast of energy at it with my mind. A tense moment passes by where nothing happens, but then I feel a strange sensation coursing through my veins. It's like electricity, buzzing and crackling under my skin. My heart races in my chest, and I can't seem to catch my breath.

Suddenly, one of the chairs shoots up into the air and spins wildly before flying off the side of the Tower.

At first, I'm afraid. I don't understand what's happening to me, and I feel like I'm losing control. But then, as the feeling intensifies, something inside me clicks into place. It's like a switch has been flipped.

It's exhilarating and terrifying all at once. I feel like I could do anything, and yet I'm afraid of what might happen if I lose control. But as I take a deep breath and focus, I feel the power beginning to stabilize. It's like I'm learning to control a new muscle, and with each passing moment, it becomes stronger and more familiar.

As the electricity fades, I look around. Everything seems different, more vibrant and alive than before. I feel like I've been awakened to a new world, and I can't wait to explore it.

Knox and Cassius look at me, a mixture of surprise and concern on their faces.

"How do you feel?" Cassius asks.

Even though I haven't moved from my spot, I feel like I've run a marathon. My chest heaves, but I'm full of excitement, practically giddy from it.

"Great," I pant with a smile. "More than great actually."

Knox's face brightens. "Can you do it again?"

Hands out, I let the energy flow through me without fear, and like before, there's a burst of electricity deep in my bones and another chair is thrown off the side of the building.

"Perfect, little dove!"

We spend the next hour practicing different exercises, trying to get me to focus my power and not make it so chaotic. Sometimes, the energy comes easily, but others, it's harder to grasp. It's frustrating to me because I want to nail it every time, especially because I started so strong, but I tell myself I need to be patient.

Even with me being hard on myself, my men are extremely calm and patient.

"You're doing great, Eve," Cassius says, giving me a reassuring smile.

"We'll keep practicing," Knox assures me.

"I just feel like there's not enough time," I say as Cassius moves the remaining chairs a little closer. "Aris can pop here any minute, and then what? I'm not ready."

"Then we take him on," Knox says.

"You're putting too much pressure on yourself," Cassius calls over to us as he steps aside. "Just relax and try again."

Trying to remember what I did before, I close my eyes, take some calming breaths in and out, and talk to myself. My words are a little more aggressive this time, but I can't help it. The urgency to get this right is a constant buzz inside me.

Come on, come on. It's up to you. You have to get this right.

I raise my hands and aim at the chairs.

This time when I force down my walls, the chaos inside me is a wild and untamable storm, flooding out of me in a rush. A resounding boom echoes, the air ripples as the power shoots out wide, and the next thing I know, the chairs and Cassius are tumbling off the rooftop.

Stomach dropping, I scream and run to the edge.

He was too close! Oh my god!

I expect to see him plummeting to his death, but when I look over the edge, I see him perched on a scaffolding a few floors below, laughing up at me. The wind tosses his hair about his face.

"That was fun!" he yells. "It's going to take more than that to kill me, Eve!"

I feel a mix of relief and anger. "That was not funny, Cassius!" I shout down at him.

He shrugs before kicking open a nearby window and leaping inside. "Hey, Dracon!" he says so loud, I can still hear it past the wind. "Stop jerking off in here!"

"I'M ON THE PHONE, CASSIUS!" Dracon's furious bellow explodes from the room he just disappeared into, followed by Cassius's hysterical laughter. "Get the fuck out of my room before I throw you out the window myself!"

I shake my head as Knox comes up to my side. He holds out a hand, and I automatically slide mine in his.

"You did great, little dove," he whispers to me and walks me back across the pool deck to one of the benches. Together, we sit. "But I think that's it for today."

He stares at me for a long time, something clearly plaguing his mind. It never leaves his lips though. So, we just sit in silence, his longer finger running across the rubber band on my wrist, as the night settles over Andover City. The lights of the neighboring buildings twinkle back at us, and I lean against him. He's stiff at first, unsure how to respond, but it isn't long before he turns and drapes an arm around me, getting comfortable.

"Little dove..." he whispers, his voice feather soft. "There's... There's something I want to talk to you about."

KNOX

I take a deep breath, trying to steady my nerves. This is it. I finally got her alone, and with the battle against Aris so close I can practically feel the universe trembling with anticipation, I know I can't keep my feelings to myself anymore. Even if I don't quite understand it fully.

I have to tell her because...well, she deserves to know.

"It's…important."

Twisting slightly, Eve looks up at me, concern etched on her face. "Is everything okay?" she asks.

I try to focus on the warmth of her skin against mine. So alive. She's so *alive.* And I'm—I'm not.

"Yes, everything is fine," I say, trying to steady my voice. "It's just that…I've been feeling something towards you. Something I've never felt before."

Confusion flickers in her eyes. "What do you mean?" she asks.

I take a deep breath, feeling my heart racing. "Little dove, I-I think I might…I might…love you."

There's a moment of silence as Eve processes my words. I can feel my heart pounding in my chest as I wait for her response.

"I don't know what to say," she finally says, her voice soft.

I can feel the rejection looming, and I try to steady myself. "I understand if you don't feel the same way," I say in a rush. "I just needed to tell you how I feel. This is just so new to me. I don't understand how humans do this kind of thing and—"

Her lips are against mine, silencing the rest of my words. Like it always does when I'm with her, my body betrays me, the hunger growing, my cock twitching to life in my pants. My hand slides behind her neck, and I draw her in closer. My tongue spears past her lips and tangles with hers, the passion growing.

My head swims. I must love her. I must. I've never

felt something as consuming and maddening as this. I'd kill for her. I'd die for her.

I've watched men do the unthinkable for a woman, and now I can be counted among them. Foolish and in love.

How pathetic.

But would I change it?

Absolutely not.

When my little dove finally pulls back, her chin tilts and I gaze into her beautiful emerald eyes. Eyes I could stare at for all eternity if she let me.

If she feels the same.

After everything I've done to her—kidnapping her, trying to kill her, almost handing her over to Opia and Brone—I wouldn't be surprised if she didn't.

I'm not sure I deserve it.

"I know how hard that was for you," she says, voice gentle.

I swallow.

Her hand touches my chest, and my heart beats faster from her nearness.

She smiles, and with the lights of the city gleaming behind her, surrounding her in an ethereal glow, I'm captured by her beauty. She may not think it, but she's perfect in every way. Perfect for me.

"You're so cute when you're nervous," she says with a little laugh.

"I'm Death," I reply automatically. "Death isn't *cute.*"

She shrugs. "Sorry to break it to you, but you very

much can be. But don't worry. Love is scary. For every-one. You're not the only person who struggles with it."

"Oh?"

She nods. "The best thing for you to do is just go with your gut. Try not to overthink it. Just...break down that inner wall you've built inside yourself, you know, to protect yourself."

Wait a fucking minute. This is starting to sound a little too familiar.

Is she using my own words against me?

She must see my realization on my face because she laughs.

"And, before I torture you any more..." She slides closer to me on the bench. "I love you too."

My next breath freezes in my lungs.

Did she just say...?

She leaves a light kiss on the tip of my nose and stands. "Thanks for the lessons today, and the advice. I'm going to try and get some sleep." Then she walks inside, where I can hear Cassius's laughter and Dracon's angry shouts the moment she opens the door.

I sit there, stunned. Not only from my little dove's confession of love to me but because of the strange situation I have found myself in. Never in a billion years had I expected to be living among humans, finding brotherhood with a demon and an Apex shifter, and falling in love with the daughter of my enemy.

Yet here I was.

And if given the chance, I wouldn't change a fucking thing.

CHAPTER ELEVEN

EVE

I'm nervous as I step out of the car and look up at the building in front of me. It's Kat's Kradle, my old job, the strip club where I used to dance. Just standing here on the sidewalk, the memories come flooding back, good and bad.

I turn to the three men who brought me here: Dracon, Cassius, and Knox.

"What are we doing here?" I ask, my heart racing.

Cassius smiles, a mischievous glint in his eye. "Just trust us, Eve. It's going to be okay."

Dracon nods in agreement, and I reluctantly follow the three of them as they lead me to the door. It's locked, but Knox pulls out a key and opens it up.

Strange… Why would he have a key?

Maybe Kat let him borrow it? If she hasn't left this city, that is.

Either way, I decide not to question it and step inside.

I'm immediately hit with the smell of fresh paint and cleaning supplies. The once dingy and dark club has been transformed into a bright and airy space that is both modern and inviting.

The walls have been painted a crisp white, and the floors have been replaced with sleek hardwood. The old stage has been torn down and replaced with a new one, complete with state-of-the-art lighting and sound equipment. The bar has been expanded, and new seating has been added, including plush leather couches and armchairs.

In the center of the room, there's a beautiful chandelier that hangs from the ceiling, casting a warm glow over everything. It's the perfect touch, adding just the right amount of elegance to the space.

But what really catches my eye is the artwork that hangs on the walls. Large, colorful murals cover the once plain and drab walls, depicting scenes of dancers in motion. It's beautiful, and I can't believe how much it adds to the space.

As I walk around the room, taking it all in, I can't help but feel excited about the future of this place. My old home.

"Oh my god," I whisper, tears welling up in my eyes. "How...Who..." I can barely speak. The last time I was here, this place was completely trashed. Destroyed. This must have taken so much time and money...

Confused and overwhelmed, I turn to my men. They're all smiling, even Knox, his hazel eyes shining with a secret he's been keeping for a long time.

"It still needs some work, but it's almost there," he says. There's a warmth on his face, the same kind I saw up on the pool deck when he said he loved me, and it makes my heart beat faster.

"And Kat?" I ask.

"Oh, she'll be running the place again. If she wants to, that is. This is her domain," Cassius explains.

I smile. "She definitely wasn't one for micro-managing."

"That's what we figured," Dracon chimes in.

"And the girls? The rooms upstairs?"

"All getting updated and brought up to code," he replies. "It's shocking this place passed any inspections."

"Oh, Kat would let the inspectors get private dances. So…yeah." Man, I miss her. And the life I used to live here, before I met the Kings. Back then, my biggest concern was making sure I hit all my cues on stage and what to do if a customer got too handsy with me or my friends.

Now I have to fight a horseman, who just happens to be my father.

Pulling out a remote from his pocket, Cassius presses a button and a deep bass, seductive song starts playing on the speakers. A raise a brow.

"Why don't you show us some of your moves? I've never been to a strip club before, so I'm not sure how it works." His grin is wicked.

Hand on my cocked hip, I stare at him in disbelief. I'm a hundred percent certain he's lying, I laugh. This is

Cassius we're talking about here–Hell demon with the libido of a jackrabbit.

He holds up his hand in defeat. "Fine, fine. I meant him." He grabs Knox by the shoulders. "He's a strip club virgin."

"Come on, Eve," Dracon says and holds out his hand for me. "Dance for us."

Taking his offer, he pulls me toward the raised stage and helps me step up. The guys pull off three chairs from the table tops, place them in the front row, and take their seats.

I take a deep breath, feeling the soft warmth of the spotlight wash over my skin. I can hear the sound of the music start to play, a slow, seductive song that makes my heart race.

Dracon, Knox, and Cassius's eyes locked on me, and I can feel their heated gazes roaming me like caresses. It sends shivers down my spine. This is a private show, just for them, and I want to make it special.

I start to move my hips, swaying to the music as I reach up and slowly start to undress, unbuttoning my blouse and hiking up my skirt to give them peeks of what lies underneath. The guys watch in awe as I reveal more and more of my body, and I can't help but feel beautiful under their gaze.

As the song continues, I keep moving, slowly stripping off my clothes until I'm left in nothing but my black lace lingerie. I move closer to the edge of the stage, feeling the heat of the spotlight on my skin as I reach out to the guys.

They stand up, making their way towards me, and I can see the desire in their eyes. I reach out to them, pulling them onto the stage with me as the music continues to play.

We dance together, moving in sync as we explore each other's bodies. Their hands slide over me, tracing over my curves as I move against them.

In that moment, I know that I'm exactly where I'm meant to be. With these men, in this club, dancing and exploring the depths of our desire together.

As the song comes to an end, we come together in a powerful embrace, our bodies entwined as we bask in the afterglow of our private show. I can feel the heat of their skin against mine, and I know that this is just the beginning of what's to come.

I can feel myself blushing, which is crazy as I adore my three Kings, and we're not shy about being intimate. Yet this is different, and I know that their affection is heightened by their primitive hunger for my body. They aren't holding back, their hands running all over my body, and I am so caught up in the moment that I can't keep track of whose hands are where. One of them is peeling down my bra strap while another unlatches it, and the third's fingers are tugging my panties down my legs until I'm wearing nothing but my heels.

And I've never been with all three at the same time where I feel their control slipping, when I doubt they'll stop, but I don't want them to—can't imagine *ever* wanting them to. Not after their incredible gift to me.

There's no pause in their touches invading every

inch of me, plucking at my nipples, sliding fingers between my pussy lips, finding my fire, lips on my neck…all over me. They are touching me everywhere all at once and I find it hard to breathe between gasps.

Flames flare through my stomach and spreads over my body and they devour me.

"So, now is the time where you all get naked," I tease, barely catching my breath. Cassius brings his mouth to mine, stealing my words, kissing me with the intensity of a madman who needs to claim what's his—me.

My toes curl when he kisses me with such passion, his tongue exploring my mouth, while Knox's mouth locks around my pussy, pushing his head closer.

Dracon has his mouth full of my breast, and I know I have to be the luckiest woman to have ever lived. I don't know what I did in a past life to deserve them.

"Are you ready for us?" Cassius sighs the words like they are the most important words he's ever spoken.

I barely have time to respond, because the three of them are stripping, but they're moving too fast. "Hey, slow down, I want to savor every moment."

Of course, my words came too late. I've now got three naked men in front of me, engorged cocks rock-hard and huge.

"Oh, you wanted to watch us?" Cassius muses sarcastically, grabbing hold of his cock, pumping his fist back and forth a few times, a hiss spilling from his lips. "There's no way we could come close to matching your beautiful dance, and right now I'm still on a high from having watched you."

"I've memorized it so I can watch it over and over in my imagination," Knox adds.

Dracon's just watching me like a starving beast about to lunge at me, and I fucking love being stared at like that. Slick gushes down my inner thighs at the filthy promise in his eyes.

Dracon leans in, his hand delicately tracing the length of my jaw, then finds the soft curve of my neck, lowering down to my chest and cupping my breast, two fingers pinching my nipple.

"I think she's ready to experience three Kings filling her."

Knox growls his approval, as if the mention of them claiming me at once turns him wild. Cassius is already laying down on his back on the stage, his cock sticking upright, so big and dripping with eagerness.

"Well, I am a virgin to being claimed by three men at once, but I am not one to avoid trying something at least once." I make a purring sound and slink down on all fours, because I can also play. In slow, deliberate motions, I slink like a cat toward Cassius. When I glance back over my shoulder, Dracon and Knox are leaning over for the perfect view of my ass and every-thing I'm showing them.

"You're glistening with desire, little dove." Knox points out the obvious.

"And? Are you just going to stand there and do nothing about it?" I'm crawling over Cassius's body, purposefully dragging my breasts across his dick, then farther up his torso as I straddle him.

Dracon and Knox are scrambling over to us, one of either side of me, their eyes hazy with arousal.

"Sit on him," Knox commands. "Show us your pussy stretching over him." Before I can even react, Cassius bucks his hips, the tip of his cock hitting me right at my entrance like they're magnets polarized to always find one another.

There's no resistance as he thrusts into me.

I cry out from his stretch and the ferocity with which he claims me, at the surprise and arousal that shoots through me. My back arches. "More, please more."

Dracon and Knox are behind me now, watching Cassius plunging deep in me. "You're so beautifully tight," he groans, his breaths racing.

"You heard our gorgeous girl," Dracon murmurs. "Let's satisfy her."

And they're on me without pause, Dracon at my rear, his hands prying my cheeks apart, his finger finding my puckered ass, teasing my hole with tiny circles.

He pushes a finger into me and I cry out—the rear entrance takes a bit to work open and Dracon knows exactly how to do it right, he uses my slickness to pump into me.

"Look what a good girl you are, your ass sucking down on my finger, wanting more. Does she want more?"

"Yes," I blurt out, just short of demanding he go

faster and either put another finger or let me feel his dick.

"You are beautiful," Cassius praises me, his lips curling into the most perfect grin. "And so perfect for us."

Knox is there, his fingers sliding across my jawline, turning my head to face him from where he's kneeling beside Cassius and leaning in.

Our mouths lock, while Dracon replaces his fingers with his erection, taking his time to push into me. The pain is delicious, a surge of energy along with lightness engulfs me.

Cassius holds me still, deep in me, and waits for Dracon to work himself in, while Knox is kissing me with a passion like the world's about to end. All this combined has me believing that fairy tale happy endings might be possible.

He breaks from me, his fingers gently stroking through my hair. "Are you ready for me?"

A moan slips past my throat as I try to respond, which is exactly when Dracon gets himself deep into me. And it's a wonderfully strange sensation to feel two massive cocks deep in me, so close they could be touching. They fill me up...and speaking of which...

Knox pushes back onto his knees, his cock bouncing up in my face.

As I lay eyes on the delicious treat in front of me, a rush of excitement and anticipation washes over me. It calls to me and my gaze feasts on the thick bulbous end, my senses fully awake, my mouth salivating. Savoring for a taste, I murmur, "Don't make a girl wait. Come to me, Knox."

And he's there, shifting closer, his cocking pushing past my lips, and I greedily take him. Inhaling slowly through my nose as I take him in, I hold Knox's gaze because I love the savage look in his eyes as I suck his cock deeper into my mouth.

I whimper as he pushes in deeper, the tip kissing the back of my throat. Tears flood my eyes, and I pull back, then work him back in. My tongue flicks him on the underside of his shaft.

Cassius and Dracon decide I have had more than enough time to adjust to them all, and they start pulling back and pushing in, slow at first as they find their pace.

Dracon has his arms wrapped around me so his fingers can apply pressure to my clit.

"Yes, please yes," I gasp through my full mouth. I don't think they can hear the words, but they get my meaning and the four of us move together harmoniously, our groans like songs, my Kings fucking me hard. Thrusting in and out, leaving me full and more adored than I've ever felt before...like I can't catch my breath from all their attention.

My body aches, my insides tightening, my pussy and ass clenching down on my men's cocks. I squeeze my lips around Knox's dick, and get the exact response I was hoping for—I love hearing them growl.

There's something magical about being fucked by these three men that leaves me feeling light, like I'm flying, like no matter what happens, they will always be by my side.

Sweating from the heat our bodies are producing from grinding and moving, my belly tightens as my orgasm crashes through me, coming like a storm, tearing me.

My body shudders, guttural moans rippling over my throat as I'm soaring through the heavens. The men never release me from their clutches and keep fucking me through my orgasm.

And I wouldn't have it any other way, because I know that tonight I'm going to be riding this euphoria ride a few more times…and I'm more than ready.

CHAPTER TWELVE

DRACON

Early the next morning, while darkness is still cloaking the skies outside the Tower windows, I creep out of my bedroom. My mind is a chaotic mess of scenarios of what we might face with Aris, and every single one leaves me shaky with anger and worry.

Worry for Eve, that is.

I need to clear my head, so I think a quick little trip to my favorite hilltop on the outskirts of Andover might be just what I need. A way to soothe the voices in my head and focus on the battle ahead.

As I reach the foyer, I can hear the gurgle of the coffee maker running and the clinking of glasses. The delicious aroma of coffee beans mixed with sugary caramel fills my nose, which is usually how Taliah makes her coffee whenever she's here on a morning errand. But why is she here? I don't remember giving her anything for today, besides the normal laundry run. And that definitely doesn't need to be done at four a.m.

When I peek into the kitchen, I find that it isn't Taliah rummaging around in the kitchen. It's Eve, still dressed in her skirt and button-down blouse from yesterday.

"Couldn't sleep?" I ask her. She nearly jumps out of her skin at the sound of my voice, breathing hard and clutching her chest.

"Jesus Christ, Dracon!" she gasps, but makes sure to keep her voice low to not disturb the others. "What if I blasted you by accident?"

I smirk. "Guess I would have deserved it then."

"You damn well would!"

Looks like I'm not the only one on edge around here.

She pours herself a mug full of the freshly brewed dark roast and adds a touch of caramel syrup. When she puts it to her lips and sips, her eyes roll back like she's in ecstasy, and images of her writhing and moaning while Cassius, Knox, and I shared her yesterday flash in my mind.

My dick twitches.

As hot as that was, something that has been plaguing me are my own damn feelings. Feelings about her.

"Tahlia introduced caramel in coffee to me, and it's heavenly," she says as she takes another sip. "You may need to give her another raise."

I chuckle. "I'll think about it."

An awkward silence stretches between us. She stares at me from over the rim of her mug and raises a brow.

"Why are you up so early? Did you want a cup too?"

I shake off her offer. "Insomnia," I half-lie. I don't want to tell her my real worries, just in case it ends up increasing her nerves. I walk around the kitchen island to close the distance between us, my heart pounding a little faster. "I know it's early, but would you be up for a little adventure?"

She puts down the coffee. "Should we wake Cassius and Knox?"

"You and me." I grab her by the arm and haul her against my chest, loving the way her eyes darken and heat builds between us.

That easily.

Eve is always easy when it comes to me and the other Kings. Ours.

Mine.

And it's time for me to take her alone.

Her palm presses against my chest and sends heat curling from the area, spiraling down into the pit of fire inside of me.

"You and me," she repeats low under her breath. "Did you want me to personally thank you for your role in fixing up the club, Dracon?"

Fuck, even the way she says my name. The syllables of it. "Maybe."

I tighten my grip on her to the point of pain, my fingertips digging into her soft skin. Eve takes it like a champ, the way she'll take my cock before too long. I can smell her lust building, along with the wetness already pooling between her legs.

"What did you have in mind?" she asks.

"I love that you're up for anything." The word clogs in the back of my throat. Love.

I want this alone time with her. I've spent years as the Apex alpha, the position rife with long hours, blood and murder, and solitude. Never a mate. Never a partner, even though the other Kings are there to try and share the burden with me.

I've never felt this way about a woman before in my long, long life.

Eve has stood by me even when she fucking hated me. Despite my broken past, she's helped me find closure.

I press a hard kiss filled with promise to her lips before releasing her, hard enough to have her struggling to find her balance. "Come."

I take her up the steps to the pool deck. It has the space I need to change shape. The need to release the animal within me builds inside, a constant ache, until the open air fills my lungs. Eve follows along obediently but it's probably the only obedience I'll get out of her today. Or ever.

Good. I stretch my arms out at my side, heart already thudding with my desire to set my predator free.

"Get over here." I point to the edge of the deck in front of me, and she quickly moves into place. Holding her gaze, I will the change and magic rips through my bloodstream turning it to pure flame. The image of my dragon form fills my head and bones crack, muscles reshaping, until the huge frame takes up the majority of the rooftop.

Exhaling, I send a puff of smoke trailing over Eve, caressing her body in a promise of things to come. She's close enough to touch my snout but hasn't moved an inch. I flash my teeth at her in clear sign for her to prepare before I wrap my claws as gently as possible around her torso. A pump of giant wings is all it takes before we're in the air.

I weave through the clouds with the precious cargo clenched in my claws, making for a hillside not too far from here with a fantastic view of the land below. The fucked-up and busy city we've all come to call home. It might be broken, but it's ours.

This close to dawn, the sky is already painted by a hint of gold although the rest of the world is still blanketed in blues and grays.

I set Eve on her feet before landing at her side and willing the change back to man, never breaking eye contact with Eve and the awe on her face.

"You come here a lot, don't you?" She turns to me in understanding.

I nod once, dipping my head. "When I need to get away. Being in the center of the city has its perks but there is…something in the quiet here."

"You're alone in your thoughts too often." She steps up to me and loops her arms around my neck. "Time for you to get back into your body."

She slides her palm down my chest, trailing down to

my crotch and the hardness already pulsing there, growing harder and thicker the longer she touches me.

Much to her eternal surprise, I grip her wrist to halt her movements. "Eve." Her name is a prayer. "I want too many things to say. And you've given me more than I ever thought possible." Why is this so goddamn hard? Three little words. That's it. I already feel them, and that should have been the hardest part—getting an ancient asshole like me to bend and drop his guard, to even get to a point where I let someone into my world.

Yet, here we stand together.

She blinks at me, her lips pursed. Waiting. Waiting for me to get on with whatever it is I want to fucking say.

"You mean the world to me," I start. "What we've built together and with the other Kings, it's everything. And I...fuck." The worlds are a growl, smoke curling from my human nose. "I love you. Okay?"

For some reason the expression comes out as a threat.

Luckily for me, she knows. She knows me better than anyone ever has, and sometimes I wonder if she knows me better than I do.

"I love you. And right now I'm going to be a mushy old fuck and tell you that I want to watch the sunrise while I take you." I release her wrist and her slow, smooth stroking of my cock through my pants resumes. "I want to see the sunlight gild you in gold while I claim your wet little cunt for myself."

Her gaze flicks up to mine and a smile teases her

lips. "Always so demanding even when you're telling me about your feelings."

"I'll tell you all about my feelings as long as I'm buried inside of you." To hide my vulnerability, I bend and kiss her, sweeping my tongue through her lips.

She tastes of a promise. Heat and life.

I deepen the kiss until she's groaning and panting in my arms and her pace on my dick falters.

"Touch me."

She dutifully rips at the button of my pants and I hear the hiss of my zipper lowering. Then her fingers are releasing my cock, smearing the precum from the head all over the length.

"I love you, too, Dracon," she manages.

A small part of me releases. A little fucking knot I barely knew existed until she said it, until I knew she returned the sentiment.

I nip her bottom lip hard enough to draw blood. "Then get on your fucking knees."

She maintains eye contact as she slowly folds and brings her lips right in line with my cock. I grip the back of her head, tangling my fingers in her hair, and guide her mouth toward the head, letting her lap around it before shoving between her lips where my tongue had been.

Guiding her down, I shove between her teeth until I hit the back of her throat. Gently fucking her face while she continues to stare up at me. She takes me like a champ, even when her eyes begin to water from the constant thrusting. Her gags are music to my ears.

Better than a thousand screams.

I fucking adore it when she chokes on my cock. I pull her off my dick and twist her around so that both her palms are planted on the earth and she's facing the view doggy style. Ready to take all of me.

She's soaked through her panties. A clear line of wetness darkens the fabric when I shove her skirt around her hips and nudge the area.

"Filthy fucking girl," I murmur, drawing her scent into my lungs and holding it there.

I shove her legs further apart and push down on her back until her ass is arched in front of me before dropping and feasting on her and running my mouth along the wet line of fabric until she gasps.

Eve moans my name and turns to look at me over her shoulder. A whisper of hair on fabric and a silent moan she tries to hide. Ignoring her, I focus on her sweet pussy, fingering her clit in demanding circles before I pull the fabric aside and slide my tongue along her slit.

Wetness pools on my tongue.

I slide my tongue into her hole, pulling out only to nip her clit before I replace my tongue with my fingers. My other hand strokes my already engorged cock.

"So fucking beautiful."

There is no one like Eve, and I know there never will be even if I live another thousand years. This time together, just the two of us, means more than I'm willing to tell her. It's enough to say the words. To let her know out loud that I love her.

Enough…for now.

"Do you want this cock inside you?" I ask as I run the head through her wetness. I already know the answer.

Her eyes meet mine again and she nods, sucking her lower lip into her mouth.

I press the head of my dick harder against her and Eve lets out an adorable yelp.

I've got my hand on the back of her neck to keep her in place. Leaning over her, I blow hot air in her ear right before I shove into her. One smooth move that has her gasping.

"Fuck me," she murmurs. Low enough I barely hear her.

She shudders under me as I thrust inside, stretching her wide and loving the way her muscles tense. I flick my hips to bring myself deeper inside of her. Buried all the way to the hilt. Then I pull out so that only the head of my cock remains inside before sliding back, hard enough for my balls to slap against her.

Her pussy pulses around me and there's only her and the desperate urge to release.

Her juices slick my cock. The feeling of her, her scent and her lust, have me hardening further.

A growl burns my throat raw as the pressure inside me increases. Reaching around, I circle her clit again before pressing it between my index and middle finger, the nub swollen.

"Are you going to come for me while I fuck you?" I ask. "You going to come on command, Eve?"

She wiggles beneath me, arching her ass higher against me like a cat in heat. Desperate for the friction.

I won't let her come until I want her to.

"Do it." I lean closer still, until I'm right next to her ear. "Come for me. Beg me to let you come."

I've never felt this way about a woman, ever, until Eve. If that's not a fucking undeserved miracle then I don't know what in this life is.

"Please," she says. Breathing heavily. "I want to come, Dracon."

I shift against her and change the angle, my dick surging into her. Playing with her clit with one hand and spanking the side of her ass raw with the other. I still once I'm nearly out of her and push forward slowly. Prolonging her torture until Eve is practically falling apart.

"Come for me."

The sun peaks over the horizon as I pump inside and she clenches around me, falling straight through her orgasm. My nerves are alight with pleasure as her heat clutches at me. I drive deeper, my dick hardening fuller until my balls pulse and I slam into her a final time. Growling. Riding my own orgasm and angling up to her insides so that the head of my cock swells, knotting, keeping my cum in place as it coats her walls.

She moans again and collapses, her pussy throbbing, my knot stretching her to her limits.

I spill the last of my cum inside just as she looks over her shoulder at me again, and there is something so dark and hungry in her gaze I know she's still not satisfied. My heart races in my ears and my lungs pump like bellows. *Rough, yes,* I think as I spank her other cheek red. Leaving more than just my seed inside her as a claiming mark, but handprints as well. Rough but perfect.

The sun casts a glow over her, her hair and skin, those perfect blowjob lips. Mine. I'll never stop being amazed by the fact, or wondering what the hell I did to deserve her.

CHAPTER THIRTEEN

EVE

*E*ve.

My eyes snap open at the sound of my name, and my heart races with the sudden awakening. I lay there for a moment, unsure if I heard anything or if it was just my imagination. But then I feel it—magic coursing just beneath my skin, invigorating me and making me feel unstoppable. I can't explain why I feel different this morning, but I'm ready to take on the world with a smile on my face.

Dracon is sleeping next to me, his muscles on show from the blanket pushed down to his waist. The memory of yesterday morning floods my mind, with Dracon confessing his love on the hilltop before flying me back to the Tower and showing me that love again in another round of mind-blowing sex. My heart flutters at the thought, and I move closer to him in his bed, under his sheets, tempted to trace his muscles with my tongue.

Eve. Come to me.

I hear it again—a buzz in my mind, calling me by name. It's not a dream, and I freeze in place as the power within me surges to life. A male voice beckons me, and I feel a purpose take hold of me.

I get out of bed.

With power sparking at my fingertips, I pull on my leggings and a loose top and step into the hallway. The voice calls to me again, and I lift my head, feeling a new determination and bravery coursing through me.

That's right, I'm waiting for you.

But then fear grips me as I realize that I've heard this voice before—when the promise of death came from my father's lips. Part of me wants to scream, but something inside me has changed, something powerful and irresistible.

So I push forward, rushing towards the voice with darkness and power swirling around me. I know I'm taking a risk, but I can't resist the call any longer. Something big is waiting for me, and I'm ready to face it head-on.

DRACON

"Eve, gorgeous." I moan, rolling over in bed toward her...but I find the mattress empty. I reach out a hand, finding her spot cold.

Frowning, I push up in bed and glance at the clock on the bedside table. It's just past nine in the morning.

I'd slept in. So, I push my legs out from under the blankets and get up, scanning the room to see Eve's clothes are gone.

I picture her in the kitchen, or with one of the other men, so I head into the bathroom. Once I'm done and emerge in the hallway, I check the other rooms. Cassius is still asleep and there is no sign of Eve.

Downstairs, I pick up my pace, searching for her as unease curls in my gut.

"Eve?" I ask as I step into the kitchen, but there's no one there. No sign of a mess from breakfast. As panic slices through me, I rush through the rest of our home, even down to the morgue where Knox is pottering about, cleaning his weapons.

"Have you seen, Eve?" I ask with a manic sound to my words.

Knox jerks his head up to me, his eyes bulging. I've seen that look flaring over his face before—just before he's about to lose this shit.

"She's missing?" he hollers.

The weapons in his grasp drop to the table with a thump and he's rushing out of the room, knocking into my shoulder on the way. "Why the fuck didn't you say something earlier?"

"Go wake up Cassius and search every inch of the Tower," I growl.

I swallow hard and hit the floor with rushed steps as I run madly through the Tower. My chest squeezes at the thought that Aris got his hands on Eve, stole her from us. Fuck, what if we're too late?

Since we brought her to our home, she's crawled into my heart, and the dread of losing her now is going to bury me.

Her gorgeous face flashes in my mind, our times together, her sweet voice, and those moans…sounds of pleasure. And for a moment, I'm back at her side, staring into her deep, piercing eyes, kissing her.

But now all I feel is the icy touch of fear tearing down my spine, leaving my head silent of her voice…a cruel silence that's destroying me.

Sprinting like a maniac, I search for her everywhere and when I come up short, I end up rewinding the security camera footage.

Heart banging against my ribcage, I pour over the video of hallway just outside my room.

Then I see her.

Breath wedges in my throat and I'm leaning forward.

She stumbles out of my bedroom, looking around like she's lost, then suddenly pauses and stares straight ahead. Next thing I know, she's bolting in that direction. I follow the other cameras through the house until she's bursting into the stairwell and darting upstairs like she's on a mission.

Her lips keep moving like she's mumbling something, but there's no sound on the cameras.

I choke on nothing but the air, glaring at her scrambling up the steps, and the moment she bursts out onto the roof, the door shuts behind her and she's gone.

In a state of panic, I quickly switch to the rooftop

cameras, only to be met with static. Frustrated, I attempt to rewind the footage in hopes of catching any suspicious activity. Although the rooftop is empty, I notice that the interference with the cameras must have occurred during the early morning hours when the sun had just risen over the horizon.

I run out of the room and up the stairs like a madman. Two steps at a time, close to losing my mind.

I burst out onto the roof.

All I can do is swing around toward the pool area on the rooftop when I spot them.

Eve and Aris.

My heart freezes over and sweat drips down the nape of my neck. He's going to kill her.

In the sunlight, they stand with their feet apart, magic sparking and glinting between them. Eve has her hands stretched out in front of her, her expression fierce and determined. But I realize that I was mistaken, and it's not Eve who is hurt, but Aris.

Suddenly, Aris stumbles backward, a growl escaping his mouth.

She has the Horseman of War in her grasp, her power extraordinary. Despite knowing her strength, I'm amazed by her ability to overpower Aris, leaving me speechless with astonishment.

And absolutely terrified he's going to kill her.

"Dracon, you took your time," Eve declares with a confident and firm voice. "This idiot summoned me while I was asleep, but I woke up with my power off the charts." Sweat glistens on her forehead, her arms trembling. "I can take him down."

"Eve, not like this," my protest bursting past my lips.

"My own daughter is mocking me, thinking she has the upper hand," Aris snarls, interrupting my thoughts, then looks my way. "We're leaving."

"No way in hell," Eve retorts, shuddering as the roof trembles beneath us. She pushes her power harder, which baffles me because I don't know how she's controlling it now so easily.

In the blink of an eye, Aris is thrown backward and lands into the swimming pool, water splashing.

Panic consumes me, and I rush toward Eve. She turns toward me with hope in her gaze, and we hurry toward each other.

In that same heartbeat, magic stings my skin and water erupts out of the pool in a tremendous explosion.

Gallons of water crash into us, throwing us both back and off our feet. Eve's crying out, and I frantically fight the deluge.

When it ends, I'm fuming and scramble to my feet, completely drenched, as is my gorgeous Eve. She's pushing her wet hair out of her face, but my attention sweeps to our enemy.

My body tenses as Aris ascends from the pool, his form menacing as he levitates. Eve steps forward, electricity crackling around her, but I hold her back, unwilling to let her face him alone.

Unease pounds into me.

"Please, you have to get out of here," she swings

toward me, her eyes full of fear. For *me*. "I can finish this once and for all." Her chest is heaving for breath, determination darkening her eyes.

I shake my head, fury burning through my veins. "He's stronger than you think. We do this with all the Kings."

I grab her arm, drawing her against me, but she's fighting me, her expression hardened.

"I don't want you hurt," she blurts, her voice speeding. "Don't you get it? He's after me, and if you stay, he'll kill you. But *I* carry his power. Dracon, it feels like I could lift the entire city; I can take him."

Fear slices through me, and her stubbornness kills me. "No, you can't do this alone, and I sure as fuck am not leaving you," I growl, my inner beast roaring within me.

I stand shoulder to shoulder with her, knowing Cassius and Knox will soon arrive at the rooftop, then we can end this asshole.

Aris raises his hand and a blast of fire energy shoots towards us. Snatching Eve around the waist, I throw us to the side just as the wall of flames slice just over my shoulder as it shoots past. It leaves behind a sharp bite over my skin that feels like acid.

We land on the pool deck, me spinning as we do so I take the brunt of the fall and Eve lands on top of me.

We get up, me dragging Eve with me, but she's shoving against me.

"Eve don't!"

Yet she charges forward with a fierce war cry, and

Aris meets her stride for stride. Their powerful clashes shake the building, threatening to bring it down. I sprint after Eve, but she's already locked in a heated battle with Aris, exchanging thunderous blows of their power.

Despite her relentless assault, Aris remains unfazed, shrugging off her attacks and retaliating with his own. Eve is thrown off her feet, battered and bruised, but she refuses to give up. Her tenacity is admirable, but I know it's time for a different approach.

The first signs of my Apex beast stir within me, and I embrace the shift. My muscles bulge, bones stretch, and in a matter of seconds, I stand in my full dragon form, scales glinting in the sunlight, razor sharp teeth glistening. A deafening roar tears through the air as my wings unfurl to their full length. It's time to end this.

Aris throws another punch of fire at Eve, and she goes flying, hitting the ground hard. She doesn't get back up, and my heart sinks with dread.

A fiery anger courses through me, and I roar, unleashing a torrent of flames at Aris. He dodges them easily, moving with unnatural speed. I charge at him, my teeth bared, and manage to claw his arm, drawing blood. But it's not enough. I want him dead.

For a moment, I turn to check on Eve, and see she's pushing up to her feet, but stumbling. Aris sees his chance and unleashes a massive ball of fire that sends me reeling backward, disoriented. All the while he darts to Eve and snatches her off the floor.

I catch myself with my wings and watch in horror as

Aris's flaming red horse descends from the heavens. He flips Eve onto the charger and mounts it, riding away with her.

It's in that same second that Knox and Cassius finally burst onto the scene, but they're too fucking late.

A surge of fury and pain envelopes me, my heart pounding in my chest. There's no time to waste. Leaving Cassius and Knox behind, I take off after Aris and Eve, determined to get her back no matter what. They'll catch up—I know they will—but my priority right now is getting to Eve.

I'll tear down the whole damn city if I have to.

CHAPTER FOURTEEN

EVE

I wake up to a nightmare. I'm on a horse, a flaming one at that, and I'm miles high up in the sky. My heart is racing and cold sweat slicks my forehead and back. Aris is riding the horse with me across his lap, and he's heading straight into dark clouds. What lies beyond them is unknown, but sizzling energy skitters across my skin, and I know that if he decides to take me out of this existence with him, I may never be able to get back.

I look around, and come to the realization that there's nowhere for me to go. I'm stuck on this horse, with no idea where we're going or what Aris has planned for me. I can't even see the ground anymore, and the only thing I can hear is the sound of the wind rushing past my ears.

Lightning cracks across the sky and I scream. It's so close, the light blinding, and I start to pray that the other two horsemen, Opia and Brone, are on their way here too. Now would be the time.

That's when I see it... The curved handle of the Mortem Blade in Aris's belt. Right there, only inches away. The only thing that can kill a horseman.

My stomach somersaults. If I could just reach it...

The lightning strikes again, making me yelp, and Aris looks down at me. He's wearing a dark expression, and I can see the glint of something in his eyes that terrifies me to the core. He thinks he's won. And maybe he has. He got both me and the blade after all.

No. I refused to give up. This isn't just about me. If Aris gets away again with the blade, he'll take out all of the horsemen. He'll destroy everything, create a war that affects everyone. It'll be a bloodbath, that is, if the universe doesn't implode from the natural imbalance first.

I have to get the Mortem Blade.

Reaching out, I go for the handle, but his hand shoots out and snatches my wrist before I can even touch it.

"Don't even think about it," he says, his voice cold and menacing. His hand begins to glow as the temperature cranks up and heat sears into my flesh. I cry out at the pain, but the bastard grins. "You're mine now, Eve. There's no escaping me."

I wrench my hand back, staring at the raised and raw flesh. The pain from a single touch is excruciating, but I try to keep my fear at bay. I don't know what he wants from me, but I know that I need to find a way out of this situation. I can't let him control me, no matter what.

As the horse continues to fly through the clouds, I sift through my options. I need to think, to come up with a plan.

The roar of a giant beast fills the air, and the clouds below us ignite in orange and red flames. Hope flares alive in my chest.

Dracon!

A flash of his dragon's wings peaks through the mist. He's still too far away, but he's getting closer, gathering speed.

When Aris glances over his shoulder and spots him, he tenses. "Time to finish this pest for good," he says, malice dripping off every word. Then, his hand shoots to the Mortem Blade, and my breath halts.

Oh no!

Fear and adrenaline pushing through my veins, I scramble to come up with my next move. I have to be smart about this, or I could be fried, like my wrist.

My wrist... *The rubber band.*

I stare at it, an idea clicking into place. An absolutely crazy one, but one that Knox would be proud of and possibly could save Dracon's life.

Anything can be used as a weapon.

Anything.

Even this simple rubber band.

In one swift motion, I rip it off, carefully swing myself to the back of the flying stead, stretch the rubber, and loop it around Aris's neck, pulling it taut.

Shocked, he rears back, clawing at the thing digging into his neck and cutting off his air. I use all my strength, even press my knee into his back for leverage, and it's not long before he's gasping and sputtering, chasing his next breath but never able to catch it.

"You asshole!" I spit, my muscles aching to hold him there. He's bucking now, swinging his head like a trapped animal. "All this power and you'll be taken out by office supplies."

I don't know how much longer I can hold on. He's too strong, so I try for the blade again, but it loosens my hold on the band enough for him to reach over his head and seize both sides of my face.

The heat hits me instantly, white-hot, burning, and the scent of signed hair and skin invades my nostrils. Screaming, I flail my arms, but the jerky movements cause me to lose my balance on the horse's rear.

As I fall, my fingers find the weapon's handle and I tug it out of the hilt. Aris bellows, a terrible, guttural sound, and leaps for it, but it's no use. The flaming horse flies off without any riders, while Aris and I are in freefall, plummeting toward the earth below.

I'm falling. Falling through the air at breakneck speed. The wind whips through my hair, stinging my eyes and pushing my cheeks back. I'm screaming, but I can't hear anything over the roar of the wind.

Below me, I see the glint of the Mortem Blade as it dives through the fog before disappearing completely.

I can see the lights of the city below growing

brighter, the buildings getting more defined the closer I get. This is it. This is how it ends. I'm going to die.

I close my eyes.

But then, suddenly, something grabs me. It's big and strong and scaly. It's Dracon, in his massive dragon form. He's caught me. I'm safe, but the aftershocks of the fall still linger, making my heart pound so hard I can feel it in my throat. My breaths come in short, sharp gasps, and I can't stop shaking.

Dracon's wings beat against the wind, and we start to rise. I'm pressed up against his chest, my arms wrapped tightly around his neck. I can feel the heat of his breath washing over me. I try not to focus on the ground anymore or how close I came to a very personal date with it, only on Dracon and the feel of him close to me. Even as scaly as he is.

A huge boom shakes the night, and the buildings around us rattle. Dracon's head snaps around, and he adjusts his wings to swing us toward it instead of away. Then, in one of the city's empty public parking lots, I see a huge circular crater in the pavement. Like a meteor had just dropped in from space.

Or a certain War horseman.

Smoke wafts from the center, obscuring our view of what's left of Aris, but I'm thankful. I'd rather not see whatever's left of him and think about how that could've been me.

We land with a thud beside it, and the momentum coupled with my shaky legs has me stumbling. The second Dracon's dragon hits the ground, he begins to shift back into his human form, and he's at my side in a flash, holding me up as everything wobbles and my head spins.

"Easy now," he says, his hands firm on me, yet gentle. His gaze roams over my face, and his brow wrinkles with concern. "He burned you."

The sound of tires screeching as they peel out slices through the nearby alley, and not even a second later, the big black SUV appears with Taliah in the driver's seat, looking panic stricken. She slams on the breaks at the edge of the lot and Knox and Cassius jump out.

"Get away from here!" Cassius shouts at her before slamming the door shut behind him. She doesn't have to be told twice. In a blink, she backs out and speeds the car around the corner and out of sight.

Cassius runs over to us, but Knox is more focused on something on the other side of the cater. The Mortem Blade—it's sticking out of the pavement like it's been driven there by a sledgehammer.

Knox races for it.

"Eve!" Cassius shouts as he reaches us. His hands are all over me, on my shoulders, under my chin, touching my hair. "Ah, fuck. Aris did this to you?"

When he accidentally touches the raw flesh on my right cheek, I wince and pull back.

"Sorry, shit. That looks like it hurts," he says.

"Yeah, it does, but it's nothing then what happened to Aris," I reply and point to the crater.

"Splat?"

Dracon nods.

"Messy but efficient," Cassius says.

"Fuck yes!" Knox shouts as he lifts the Mortem Blade into the air in triumph. "Back where it rightfully belongs. With me."

"Why don't you marry it?" Cassius says playfully. "Come on, Eve. Let's get you fixed up. Maybe Talon has something to help speed up healing and—"

"Wait." Dracon throws out an arm to stop us from moving. We both glance at him to find his nostrils flaring and every muscle in his massive body tensing.

He turns slowly, and we follow his gaze to the dark figure outlined in the smoke as it rises out of the crater.

"No fucking way…" Cassius breathes in disbelief. I'm stunned into silence, while a growl rumbles in Dracon's throat.

There's no way.

There's no fucking way… He hit the ground from like six miles in the air. That's fatal.

Shit, we're in a lot more trouble than we originally thought.

CASSIUS

No normal living being could've survived a crashlanding like that. No one. Not even me or Drac, but then again, Aris is practically a god.

That only ups the ante and confirms the kind of monster we're dealing with here. We're going to have to up our game to kill this bastard, but unfortunately for him, I don't mind it when things get messy.

As the smoke clears, Aris steps out of the crater, a massive gash across his face, head bashed in on the side, and right arm hanging limply. He may be banged up, but as his head lifts and his eyes lock on Eve, I can see his body healing itself rapidly. Faster than anything Dracon or I can do.

When his arm pops back into place with an audible crack, Eve winces and shifts a little closer to Dracon. There is one mark that doesn't seem to fade on Aris though—a distinct red line across his throat.

How did that happen?

"Run, Eve," Dracon says, his Apex magic already making his skin rippled and bubble. She doesn't hesitate. She's off and running in the next second.

I don't even get to see where she hides because a battle cry rings out, and I whirl around to see Knox leaping through the air, Mortem Blade slicing the air at a deadly speed.

Aris spins just as fast, whipping his flaming sword out of thin air. Their blades meet in a flare of red flame and blue sparks, which ignite the entire street in light.

At a safe distance, Dracon and I watch as Knox faces off with his Mortem Blade against Aris. Aris's flames lick at the blade, but Knox remains unfazed, driven by his hatred and need for revenge. He's a master with the weapon, and I've seen him take down countless foes with it before. I have faith in his abilities, but there's always a sense of trepidation that comes with any fight against someone with powers as potent as Aris's.

As they circle each other, Knox lunges forward with a quick strike. Aris dodges, but not quite fast enough. The Mortem Blade grazes his arm, the metal clinking against the sword's sharp edge but unable to make even a dent. Aris growls in frustration and unleashes flames all over his body. The intensity of the heat is stifling—and coming from a demon from Hell, that means something. It makes me and Dracon backpedal, shielding our faces from the blaze.

But Knox is undeterred. He presses the attack, swinging the Mortem Blade in a wide arc. Aris retaliates with a burst of flame, but Knox deftly dodges and counters with a thrust of the blade. Again, Aris's armor takes the brunt of the blow, but the impact sends him stumbling back.

With that armor, Knox may never be able to land the death blow we need.

Dracon must've read my mind because he throws himself onto all fours as fur sprouts and his nose expands into a snout and sharp chomping jaws. He's shifted into a massive wolf.

Wasting no time, he leaps into action and charges at Aris, his fangs bared. Aris is taken off guard as Dracon tears into the armored plates on his leg with savage ferocity. I watch in amazement as the two of them grapple, each trying to gain the upper hand. The black shadows of Knox's souls shoot out, wrapping around Aris's arm to hold back his weapon, but somehow he's still able to dodge Knox's blows. Jerking his leg, he dislodges Dracon and stomps on his foot so hard, the audible crunch of bones hits my ear, followed by the wolf's whimper of pain.

Somehow, he breaks free of the soul's hold on his arm and slices the air, cutting into Knox's shoulder, who bellows in untamed fury.

My demon rises without warning, urging me to let it out. Instinctually, my hand flies to my pocket, grabbing for my snuff tin, but as I pull it out, I realize I'm not going to suppress him this time. If there ever was a time to let it free, it's now.

I chuck the tin, the thing clattering somewhere in the darkness. Then, turning back to the battle, I grit my teeth and give in, feeling the demon's power surge through me.

I charge forward, my speed and strength enhanced by the demon's influence. I can feel its hunger for battle, its desire to see our foes fall before us.

Together, the three of us battle Aris with everything we have. We move in tandem, each of us covering the other's weaknesses. Knox's Mortem Blade glimmering in the firelight, Dracon's fangs glinting in the shadows, and I move like the wind, landing punches that would dent a human's skull.

But Aris is too strong. He's a force to be reckoned with, and no matter how hard we fight, he seems to be getting the better of us. The flames around his form burn hotter, forcing Dracon back, and his blows land with greater force. He manages to jab an elbow in my gut, and all the breath is forced out of my lungs by the single strike.

He spins, simultaneously locking weapons with Knox and swiping out my legs from underneath me so that I fall onto my ass.

Fuck, I've fought and killed so many raging assholes, supernatural and non, but this guy's making me look like a fumbling amateur.

My demon snarls inside me, urging me to fight back harder, but I can feel my strength waning. Dracon and Knox aren't faring much better. They're both injured, bleeding from countless wounds, but they refuse to give up, fighting on with all the ferocity they can muster. I jump back into the fray too, kicking Aris square in the back hard enough to send him stumbling forward. Dracon takes the opportunity to latch onto the uncovered part of his thigh, biting down hard, despite the flames singing his fur. Aris's scream echoes throughout the city streets.

As his sword changes course, swinging at Dracon, Knox drops to his knees to block the blow just in time.

As we continue to battle, I feel a sense of desperation growing inside me. Even though our enemy is only a single man, it's like we're still outnumbered, outgunned, and outmatched. Like we're facing down all of the other gangs in Andover at the same time. My muscles ache, and for the first time in my entire existence, I start to question if we can really win this one.

Under our feet, the ground starts to tremble. Slightly at first, almost undetectable, but then the shaking grows to a terrifying earthquake, making the buildings surrounding the lot quake and the dust rise into the air.

My gaze whips around. Eve's crossing the parking lot, hands out, eyes focused, hair flying wildly as her power grows. The air all around her sparks and crackles, and the hair lifts on my arms.

Her power surges through the air, blasting into Aris with incredible force. He staggers, caught off guard, but it's not enough to knock him off his feet.

A delighted smile curls Aris's face. "Ah," he says slowly, "there's my daughter. The true daughter of chaos."

"That's right, Daddy. And I'm going to be the one to kill you." Her voice booms, amplified by the magic radiating off her in waves.

"Get away from here, little dove!" Knox shouts.

"No! I'm done running." Taking another step closer to Aris, she shoots another warning blast at him, knocking all of us back a step.

She's quite a sight to behold, seeing her unleash her chaos energy in such a powerful way, confident in herself and her new abilities. And ready to end this once and for all.

"Last chance, Aris. Surrender."

"Or what? You'll bring down the world around me?" He laughs. "Go ahead. You'll be helping me skip a step."

"Fine, have it your way then." Eve draws in a deep breath, and the world seems to do the same. The air around her shudders, and in a wave, appears to move back before moving *through* her body and exploding outward, through her palms. The power is so immense, I'm thrown clear off my feet, spinning through the air until I hit the ground feet away and roll to a halt. My skin stings and burns, not just from Aris's fire but from a severe case of road rash, and when I hear groaning nearby, I know I wasn't the only one hit by Eve's blast.

Dracon's lying butt-naked, face down, back blackened and scraped up pretty damn bad.

And there's Aris, on his knees, his fire snuffed out and half of his armor in tatters. But he laughs manically, his shoulders bouncing as blood leaks from his nose.

"You really thought that could kill me?" he says between spurts. "You are only *half* of me, child! Half horseman, half weak and pathetic human scrum. I made you. I was going to let you join me, but now you'll die, just like the rest of them."

Crossing her arms, Eve appears unbothered by his words. She cocks her hip, her cockiness hot as hell.

"No one can destroy me. I am destruction. I am bloodshed. I. Am. War!"

"And I am a distraction," she says.

The shadows near Aris lift suddenly, revealing Knox and a blaze of blue light cutting across the darkness.

I don't even see the final blow—it happens too fast—but when Knox kicks Aris's body, his head separates from his neck, both parts hitting the ground with a thud.

It's a gruesome sight, but also a satisfying one.

I almost can't believe it. We've won.

Eve hurries over to Dracon. I crawl over to him too

and help her roll him over. He groans, bleeding from a cut on his eyebrow and a chunk of his hair burned away, but he's alive.

"Sorry about that, but I had to get him focused on me—" she starts as Dracon sits up.

"And monologuing," I chuckle. "No need to apologize, beautiful. You did amazing. And besides, Drac's used to a little pain, right Drac?" I slap his shoulder hard and watch him wince.

"Fuck you," he grumbles.

A second later, Knox walks over, holding Aris's severed head by the hair. Blood drips from his neck, and his eyes are still wide, frozen in shock.

"Oh no! Get that thing away from me," Eve says, shooing Knox away.

His head tilts to the side as he gives her a puzzled look. "What? You don't want it as a trophy?"

"What? No! A trophy? Are you insane?"

"Very well. I'll take it then." Knox shrugs like there's nothing unusual at all about wanting to keep the head of your enemy as a prize. For him, this kind of shit happens all the time. It's why I never check the storage lockers in his morgue. Who knows what I'd find in there.

Or better yet, *who* I'd find.

Suddenly, a car's headlights flood the parking lot with light, and when we all turn around, we spot the SUV zooming towards us. It hops the curb before stopping.

Rolling down the window, Taliah sticks her head

out. "Everything alright? I was doing laps when I felt the ground shake. I swear we just had an earthquake or something."

"Nope, didn't feel a thing," I say with a chuckle. "Anyone else?"

"Not a thing," Eve replies without missing a beat.

"An earthquake? I don't think so," Knox plays along.

"Hmm…" But when Taliah's gaze roams over us, her eyes narrow in disbelief. "Right."

We all take our time rising to stand on wobbly legs and walk to the car.

"Just get us home," Dracon says and opens the passenger door with a grunt.

"One of those, 'better if I don't know' kinda things?"

"Exactly."

"You wouldn't believe us even if we told you," Eve says, climbing into the back first. I follow behind her and then Knox climbs in before shutting the door.

Taliah glances in the rearview mirror at us, taking in all our scrapes and bruises up close. That's when she sees Aris's severed head in Knox's lap and her grip on the steering wheel tightens.

"Just…don't get blood on the upholstery, okay? That shit's hard to get out."

He nods.

Then, without batting an eye, she backs the car out of the lot and whips the SUV onto the street, in the direction of the Tower, our home.

CHAPTER FIFTEEN

EVE

I sink into the soft cushions of the couch, feeling the warmth of the sun streaming through the window as I settle in for a lazy Sunday afternoon. Dracon is pressed up against me, while Cassius is pouring himself a drink at the bar. Knox, on the other hand, sits on the couch's armrest, his leg against me, making sure he's always touching me.

It's been a week since we defeated my father, the Horseman of War, Aris. Just saying it in my mind feels strange. Part of me wonders if I ought to miss Aris…he was my father after all. But how can I miss someone who's only shown me hatred?

"I can't believe it's really over," I murmur suddenly. "It feels like it was all a dream."

A wistful smile plays at the corners of Dracon's lips. "I know what you mean. But we did it. We saved you, and us, and the world."

Cassius chimes in, "And we can just enjoy life, party,

and fuck endlessly. But now that all this craziness is over, I propose we also go on a holiday."

"I've always wanted to go to the Bermuda Triangle," pipes up Knox.

"No," the three of us answer in unison, then break into a laugh. "We finally escaped danger, and you want to tempt fate again?" Cassius barks from across the living room.

It all still feels surreal to me. I never thought I'd be able to stand up to Aris and emerge victorious.

But even as they joke and laugh, I can't shake the feeling of unease that lingers at the back of my mind because I know that there's still the outstanding issue of the other two horsemen.

"Seriously though," I start. "Isn't it strange that Opia and Brone haven't shown up? It's been a whole week."

Dracon shrugs. "Maybe they've come to their senses and realize with Aris gone, the energies have been realigned once more."

"Not sure it works that way," Knox corrects, staring down at me, heartache in his eyes, and that crumbling feeling crashes through me.

As if on cue, the sound of hooves echo through the air. I sit up, alert, as do my men, scanning the window, searching for the source of the noise. And then, out of nowhere, two steeds with riders descend from the heavens and onto our balcony.

Opia and Brone had arrived.

My heart sinks. My breaths come out ragged and uneven while Knox goes to let them in. We're all on our feet, Cassius and Dracon on either side of me like they sense this isn't going to go down well for me.

My mind races as I try to think of a way to get away, but I know deep down that there's no way out. It feels like I'm trapped in a never-ending cycle of danger and fear, and that no matter what I do, I can never be truly safe.

The ominous sensation continues to rise, like a dark cloud encasing me in its shadow.

"We were wondering where you've gotten to," Knox jokes, but no one's laughing as he slides open the glass door to the balcony.

Brone as the Horseman of Pestilence is enough to fill me with a sense of dread as he enters with a slow, deliberate pace, taking in his surroundings. His almost white eyes leave me uneasy, and it makes me wonder if they're that way because he's seen too much suffering in the world. He wears dark and tattered clothes as though he's been traveling through disease-ravaged lands.

Opia pushes ahead of him, seeming to absorb the light from the room, casting her in a shadowy aura that only deepens her regal features. Her movements are graceful and fluid, like a predator stalking its prey. She wears a black riding outfit that clings to her lithe body, and her eyes scan the room with a cold intensity.

The air of menace about them both is impossible to ignore. They carry themselves like warriors, ready to do battle at a moment's notice. I remind myself that I'm one of them, as is Knox, yet I couldn't feel more different.

Under their scrutiny, a shiver runs the length of my spine.

Opia and Brone smile, which is a slightly disturbing expression on each of their faces, though for vastly different reasons. Then Brone says, "We were delayed by a disaster in another galaxy, so we came as fast as we could."

They pause in front of me, which has me nervous as hell. "You are now one of us, Eve, taking Aris's position," Opia explains. "A Horseman of Chaos, empowered to spread chaos and destruction throughout the cosmos in the means of protecting those who deserve it."

A quiver skitters down my arms, both exhilarated and terrified at the same time. I am now a creature of darkness, a harbinger of chaos and destruction, yet I'm not too sure what that means.

Around me, my men stare at me in awe, astonishment glinting in their gazes. Knox stands tall, his chin high, almost proud of me. Yet, I'm scared on the inside about what this exactly entails.

"Wow, okay. It's a bit much, but thank you," I say, my voice barely above a whisper.

Opia and Brone exchange a confused look before turning to face me, Brone continuing. "As a horseman, you have responsibility to learn exactly what that involves, so you and Knox will accompany us so we can teach you everything."

"Where we will be the four horsemen once more, unstoppable against any force," Opia commands.

And there it is...the other shoe dropping. "I-I'm not

going anywhere." I keep my voice firm. "I am going to remain on Earth."

Panic races through me, my heart thumping in my chest. We barely defeated one horseman, so we stand no chance against two of them if they decide they need to force me to go with them. Glancing around the room, I'm surprised to find Knox is gone... Great. The one person who could weigh in on this conversation vanishes.

Opia's face darkens, and she takes a step forward, her eyes glowing with a dangerous light. "You dare to refuse us?" she says, her voice laced with anger.

Brone places a hand on her shoulder, trying to calm her down. "Opia, please. Let's not do anything rash."

But Opia isn't listening. Her eyes are blazing with fury. "You're making a big mistake, mortal," she patronizes me, her voice low and menacing. "You have been given an opportunity that most humans could only dream of, and you are throwing it away."

I take a step back, Dracon and Cassius remaining close, their bodies tense as if readying for a battle.

Dracon's gaze narrows. "You heard her. She doesn't want to do this. Leave her alone."

Opia snarls, her eyes flickering with a dangerous light. "You think you can stand up to us, Apex?" she speaks firmly, her voice filled with contempt.

Dracon doesn't back down. "We'll do whatever it takes to protect her."

"Her kind isn't made to live on Earth, you understand that, Apex?" Opia snaps, her gaze burning into

Dracon. "We are meant to float through the cosmos and tend to all matters across the galaxies. To remain on one planet is lackluster in comparison."

"Maybe times are changing," Cassius pipes up. "You aren't taking her from us. We almost lost everything to keep her from that other jackass, so fuck off."

Opia's upper lip curls up and over her teeth, her threat palpable. "You have been appointed as the Horseman of Chaos, and you want to play girlfriend to your boyfriends instead?"

Her arrogance is rubbing me the wrong way, but I'm no fool and know that Opia and Brone are extraordinarily powerful, so I need to be careful.

"That's my choice. I won't leave because I have a life here. And I will help those on Earth. I'd like to think I've learned enough from Knox already."

Brone scoffs. "Highly unlikely."

"Knox survived here for centuries. It's proof your kind can coexist with humans," Dracon pipes in.

"No one can know who you are," Brone mutters, his voice laced with a threat. "It can bring disaster and tip the balance again."

"We'll protect her," Cassius announces loudly, his shoulders shooting back with determination. "Keep her identity private."

Opia's eyes narrow just as Knox's voice booms across the room. "Your business is done here, Opia and Brone." His expression is serious, and my heart thunders at what he's carrying in his hand.

He tosses Aris's head across the floor, the gruesome

blue frozen thing rolling and coming to a stop right at Opia's feet. "It's resolved," he says, his voice grave. "Eve is powerful and has me for her training. She eliminated Aris, which is proof enough for you to be on your merry way."

Momentarily speechless, my mouth falls open at the sight of Aris's head. "Where have you been keeping that?" I manage to blurt out.

Knox glances in my direction, his expression softening for a brief moment. "I kept it in the freezer for such an occasion."

Cassius interjects with a growl. "You better not have kept that in our kitchen freezer where I keep my popsicles."

"Relax," Knox answers. "I stored it down in the morgue freezer."

Dracon rolls his eyes, while Opia and Brone struggle to make sense of the conversion, if their perplexed expressions are anything to go by.

Silence falls over the room as everyone stares at the frozen head, processing the unexpected.

"It's not something we anticipated," Opia finally speaks up, her voice betraying her surprise.

Taking charge, Knox steps forward and takes a deep breath before addressing the group. "Eve and I will reside on Earth and travel wherever we're needed when called upon. It's a fair compromise."

Brone offers his input, "This is highly unconventional."

"But doable," Knox explains.

My heart leaps with excitement at Knox's proposal. The thought of living on Earth with him and traveling together to fight for our cause fills me with hope. I glance around the room, eager to see the others' reactions.

Opia raises an eyebrow, considering Knox's plan, then glances at me. "Are you certain this is what you want?"

"Yes," I answer immediately, hope flooding through me.

Brone smiles softly, his eyes shining with newfound optimism. And despite Opia grumbling, she seems to be coming around to the idea.

"It's a risk, but I suppose it's worth a try," she says, surprising me with her openness to the idea. "Anything goes wrong, just know that you will be held account- able, Knox."

"I accept the terms," he states with a grin and walks them out onto the balcony. Only at the doorway, does Opia turn back and glance my way. "We will be watching you, because something tells me your power is a lot more extraordinary than any of ours."

Her words worry me, but that worry doesn't last long as I watch them scale their horses and begin to ascend. They vanish in moments.

I turn to Knox, beaming with gratitude. "Thank you," I say, my voice full of emotion. A sense of relief washes over me. "We'll make this work, and you'll have to catch me up on what duty we'll get called on, but I couldn't be happier."

Dracon and Cassius take my hands, squeezing them, and my attention is on Knox's eyes, sparkling with joy.

With the two horsemen gone, I throw myself at Knox, Cassius and Dracon closing in, and we're in one big group hug.

Leaning against my men, I feel a rush of gratitude and love for them all. "I was sweating big-time just then. Knox, you did amazing, thank you."

"Yeah man, you knocked it out of the park," Cassius states. "Just get rid of that fucking head."

Dracon's patting Knox on the shoulder. "I'm proud of you."

"And I damn love all three of you. Nothing is going to separate us." Tears prick my eyes as I think about how much the three Kings mean to me. They've been my rock, my constant support.

They draw me closer, wrapping me in their arms, and I know that no matter what challenges lie ahead, as long as we have each other, we can overcome anything.

EPILOGUE

EVE

I dive into the cool water, feeling the rush of the current against my skin. The sun beats down on my back, but the water is refreshing, and I feel weightless as I swim to the other end of the pool. When I reach the edge, I push myself up, my arms feeling heavy from the effort.

As I pull myself out of the water, I look up and admire the top stories of the Tower. They're finally finished and no longer under construction. The view from up there must be amazing. I smile to myself, glad that we've come so far.

"Cannonball!" Cassius shouts as he jumps into the water, splashing me with a wave. I laugh and splash him back, enjoying the coolness of the water on my skin.

Knox is sitting under an umbrella, enjoying the shade. He's never been too keen on the sun, which Cassius teases him mercilessly for, but he's content watching us play in the water.

Dracon comes over with a drink, handing it to me as I sit on the pool stairs. I'm happy with my three men, loving them all, and they all love me too. It's a strange thing, to love more than one person, but it feels natural to me. They each bring something unique to our relationship, and I wouldn't want it any other way.

We continue talking, laughing, and enjoying each other's company. It's moments like these that make everything we've been through worth it. We've come so far, and I'm proud of us.

As the sun starts to set, we dry off, and Cassius turns to me with a grin. "Remember when you almost took down Aris with that rubber band?"

I chuckle, "Hey, anything can be used as a weapon." I glance at Knox with a smile. "A death expert taught me that."

Cassius modifies his voice to act as a news reporter and holds up his fist as a pretend microphone. "The mighty Aris, Horseman of War, has been taken out by a piece of office stationery."

To my surprise, Knox snorts a laugh.

Cassius changes the subject. "So, what do you guys want to do tonight?"

"Maybe watch a movie? We can order some food and have a night in." Dracon suggests. "We deserve the break."

Knox nods in agreement, "I'm not in the mood to go out tonight."

I smile. "That sounds perfect. I'll order some food and we can pick out a movie."

"I have the *perfect* one," Cassius says with a wicked grin and hurries out of the pool to towel off. "I'll meet you all inside."

Chucking the damp towel at Knox's face, he rushes off.

"I swear to fuck, if he makes us watch *Constantine* again…" Dracon huffs, "I'm going to rip his legs off."

We head inside, and I order some pizza and drinks for us. While we wait for the food, Cassius readies the movie while we all take our places on the couch. It's comfortable, almost normal, and I feel lucky to have these three amazing men in my life.

"I really don't think I can handle a horror movie," I say, digging my hand in the popcorn bowl.

"Don't worry. It's nothing scary," he replies with a grin.

"Rom com?"

"Not exactly."

"Can you shut up and put the damn thing on?" Dracon growls.

Cassius obliges, pressing the play button on the remote and leaning back into the cushions.

When my bedroom flashes on the screen, then my face, and finally my body, with my hand in between my legs, every inch of me hunches over in embarrassment.

Oh no… I know *exactly* what movie Cassius picked, and right now, I'd gladly take *Constantine* for the millionth time over this.

In the video, I'm grabbing my breast and pinching my nipple, while my other hand plays with my clit, teasing my folds, and dipping in and out of my wet pussy. Video me's eyes meet with mine, and I remember the anger I see there, wanting to give Cassius, Dracon, and Knox a show.

And boy, was I regretting that decision.

Looks like I was never going to live this one down, was I?

The last time Cassius had put this video on, we ended up fucking on the couch like a real porno.

On the screen, my back arches, my moans flowing from my lips as the ecstasy builds, and heat pools between my legs. Slowly, I turn to the Kings, only to find each of them staring at me with fire in their eyes.

Oh shit…

"Told you it was my favorite movie," Cassius says, his voice a rumble of primal need. His hard cock is already tenting his pants, and I try to swallow past the tightness in my throat.

My clit throbs, knowing exactly what's coming next.

I'm in trouble. Deep, delicious trouble.

"Come here, little dove," Knox coos, eyes glowing.

I jump to my feet, popcorn flying everywhere, and at the same time, hands grab me, my towel and swimsuit ripped off my body in a flash. Laughing, I'm dragged back down onto the couch as Cassius, Dracon, and Knox pounce on me, their kisses searing, their touches rough and needy.

And I let them own me, body, heart, and soul. Like I have before and like I hope to do for the rest of eternity.

My Kings of Eden.

Because being with them isn't just Heaven and Hell and everything in between.

It's paradise.

Demons are real.

They say never enter into a deal with them, but what if I had no choice?

What if they are three of the most gorgeous men I've seen my entire life?

And what if my lesson to learn here is that no matter how attracted I am to them, how much I yearn to kiss them, I'm in danger.

But my life's never been the easiest. I've bounced from house to house, living in foster care, with no true place to call home.

And there's an ancient darkness that follows me around where I go.

They may be demons, but I'm no angel, and this darkness craves the Hell they give.

Or maybe I've just been damned from the start.

ABOUT MILA YOUNG

Best-selling author, Mila Young tackles everything with the zeal and bravado of the fairytale heroes she grew up reading about. She slays monsters, real and imaginary, like there's no tomorrow. By day she rocks a keyboard as a marketing extraordinaire. At night she battles with her mighty pen-sword, creating fairytale retellings, and sexy ever after tales. In her spare time, she loves pretending she's a mighty warrior, walks on the beach with her dogs, cuddling up with her cats, and devouring every fantasy tale she can get her pinkies on.

Ready to read more and more from Mila Young?
www.subscribepage.com/milayoung

For more information...
mila@milayoungbooks.com

ABOUT HARPER A. BROOKS

Harper A. Brooks lives in a small town on the New Jersey shore. Even though classic authors have always filled her bookshelves, she finds her writing muse drawn to the dark, magical, and romantic. But when she isn't creating entire worlds with sexy shifters or legendary love stories, you can find her either with a good cup of coffee in hand or at home snuggling with her furry, four-legged son, Sammy.

RONE AWARD WINNER
USA TODAY BESTSELLING AUTHOR
INTERNATIONAL BESTSELLING AUTHOR

Join Harper's reader group for exclusive content, sneak-peeks, giveaways, and more!